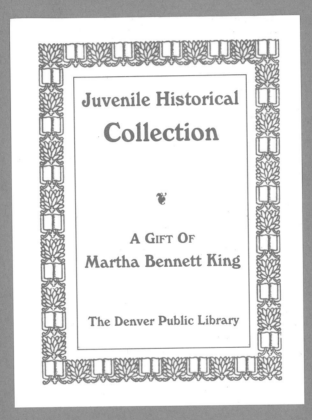

by LOCH
and by LIN

By Sorche Nic Leodhas

By Loch and by Lin
    Tales from Scottish Ballads
The Laird of Cockpen
Kellyburn Braes
Sea-Spell and Moor-Magic
    Tales of the Western Isles
Claymore and Kilt
    Tales of Scottish Kings and Castles
Always Room for One More
Ghosts Go Haunting
Gaelic Ghosts
All in the Morning Early
Thistle and Thyme
    Tales and Legends of Scotland
Heather and Broom
    Tales of the Scottish Highlands

by LOCH and by LIN

Tales from Scottish Ballads
by SORCHE NIC LEODHAS
illustrated by VERA BOCK

HOLT, RINEHART AND WINSTON
New York   Chicago   San Francisco

FOR ANN DURELL

This book of ballad stories
    with
the *Beannachd baird**

> *"Sona bithid tu*
>   *Agus eiridh gu math dhuit*
>   *Fad finn foinneach an latha."*

*the bard's blessing

"Happy shall you be
And it shall be well with thee
All the livelong day."

Contents

Introduction

EVERY ballad tells the story of something that actually happened long ago. Sometimes the event was great enough to be famous in history, so that we find battles, deeds of kings and nobles, intrigues, and high romance celebrated in these old songs. Even more often, however, the ballad maker wrote his ballads to tell his small world about the doings of persons not at all important except in the villages or shires in which they lived. Thus the popular ballads of Scotland are the songs of the common folk, first made by one of themselves, couched in the language that they themselves spoke, telling about events which, if they had not witnessed them, they at least knew by hearsay.

The men who created these ballads were less concerned with presenting a true picture than they were with making a grand story of the happening. They drew upon their imaginations to give color to the telling, and in consequence events became more exciting, the background brighter, and the characters larger than life.

As the ballads passed down through the years each singer added a few ideas of his own, so that every ballad finally came to have almost as many versions as there were ballad singers to sing them, but in every case the original event that caused it to be written, however vague it became through use and years, was never lost sight of, and still provided the framework for the song.

That these are in truth the songs of the people is proved by the way the persons in them behave. To a Scottish crofter or village dweller, kings and nobles, in spite of their high estate, are only men, after all, and the ballad maker when telling about them made them act as his listeners would have done themselves. The Scottish kings always seemed to be closer to their people than were the kings of other lands. The basic idea of the clan —that all the members of it were kinfolk, springing from a common ancestor—may have had something to do with it. But a large number of the Scottish kings went about among their people and knew them well, and in turn were well known by them. There was no undue familiarity in the people's attitude toward their sovereigns, but their subjects, although they esteemed and honored their kings and often loved them, still thought of them as men.

So we have kings in the ballads who behave exactly as the common folk do themselves. The king in "The Tale of the Lochmaben Harper" strolls out of his castle of Carlisle, and meeting the harper, sends him to stable his old gray mare beside the king's favorite steed. The Laird of Hutton Hall, in "The Tale of Dick o' the Cow," does not hesitate to haggle with his fool over the price of the stolen steed; the Earl of Mar (a very great earl indeed), after forgiving his daughter, is on good terms with her in a very cozy fashion. "They visit back and forth." Lang Johnnie Mor and his companions, in "The Tale of Lang Johnnie Mor," walk into the castle without ceremony and frighten the king out of his wits by their size. No doubt they were enormous men, but not as large as they were made out to be by the ballad maker. Nevertheless, there were many huge men in the old days. Sir John of Erskine Park, whom Jock o' Noth mentions, was, according to history, over eight feet tall. Then there was Scotland's greatest hero, Sir William Wallace, who wielded a sword that was seven feet long. Wallace's sword is still in existence, and I understand is kept in the armory of Stirling Castle. In "The Tale of the Knight and the Shepherd Lass," the lass is unusually bold in her actions and forthright in her speech for a king's daughter, although, to be sure, she is passing herself off as a tender of sheep. In the same story, the king, like any householder, comes down and opens the door himself when the lass tirls at the pin. The common folk accepted such behavior without question. It was just what they would have done themselves.

The first two tales in this collection were taken from ancient lays, or Scottish bards' tales. They antedate the introduction of printing into Scotland by several hundred years. They are a true part of the oral tradition of the country and have always been handed down in Gaelic and in the form of verse. I have never heard nor seen a story taken from any of the lays. The other stories in the collection are not so old. They are made from ballads such as those which used to be printed crudely on leaflets or single sheets, sometimes called broadsides, and pinned up for sale on the posts of stalls at markets and at fairs. The seller often gave his potential purchasers a taste of his wares by singing them, fitting the words to old familiar airs. Few of the old ballads had musical notations of their own, but borrowed any tune that pleased them that would fit their words. These are the "twopenny ballads" whose passing Thomas Hood laments in "Hood's Own, the Comic Annual" (1838), and the ballads upon which the tales in this collection are based were very old in Hood's time, and were probably composed in the seventeenth and eighteenth centuries.

The Tale of the
Lay of the Smithy

K NOW then, all who listen, that in the beginning the Finne, the noble company of Finn, had neither swords nor lances. Shields they had, fashioned of cowhide stretched upon frames of willow withes, and helmets and arm protectors of leather. Gold they had, also, cunningly worked by craftsmen among them into rings and chains and other ornaments, and the secret of making colored enamels was known to them. But for weapons the Finne had naught but *tunnachen,* or pointed wooden poles and staves, hardened in the fire. The craft of the blacksmith was not known then in the land of the Finne.

Then upon a fair day a company of the Finne lay resting from the hunt on thick heaps of rushes strewn about the edge of the *machair,* that grassland above the shore

of the sea. Six of them there were, and they were Osein, Coilte, Diarmid, Osgar the son of Osein, Goll MacMorna, and the fair Finn MacChumhail himself.

While they lay, idly talking, there came a *bean-gruagach,* a giant woman, walking under the waters along the sands at the bottom of the sea. When she reached the shallows she came striding up through the white-topped waves that broke upon the shore.

Finn and his company rose and stood together to watch her as she came up from the sea. Although she was a giant, it was not her size that made the flesh of the heroes creep with horror. She was but little taller than the Finne, who were themselves big men. It was her ugliness, which was beyond believing, from which they shrank.

The yellow hair that sprang from her head was coarse, and spiky like an old thorn bush, and every hair stood quivering on end. She had but one eye and that one in the middle of her forehead, encircled by long matted dark eyelashes, and a black furry eyebrow overhung the eye. Her nostrils were broad and flat and flaring, like the snout of a boar, her teeth the length of a grown man's finger, and from each corner of her wide mouth projected a long sharp fang, and her skin was scaly like that of a fish.

Upon her back she bore an anvil, strapped to her shoulders by stout woven bands that crossed upon her breast and were wound thrice about her waist. Through the bands were thrust a great heavy hammer, a bellows, and a pair of tongs.

Finn, for the sake of courtesy, hid his loathing and spoke to the creature as she came toward him.

"Who are you, stranger?" he asked. "Whence have you come and what brings you to the land of Finne, O woman from the sea?"

"I am known as the *uallach gobhain,* the blacksmith to whom all the smithy's mysteries are known. My name is Lon Lonnrach, and I am the daughter of the Yellow Muilearteach. I have come here from Lochlan, that far country across the surging sea, to set up for myself a smithy where I shall forge weapons such as your eyes have ne'er beheld."

"Shall my eyes not behold them now, then?" asked Finn. "We will come with you to see you set up your smithy."

"That you will not if I can help it!" said the giant woman, and turning away from Finn she hastened across the plain, and her feet sped so swiftly that soon she was out of sight. But the Finne lost no time in taking up her trail, following where her footprints led.

Over the machair and over the moor strode the bean-gruagach, Lon Lonnrach. She leaped up the yellow hill beyond the plain and down the other side. She climbed up and down a green hill and a brown hill, but her feet did not falter on the way. Then she came to a hill that was neither yellow nor green, nor was it brown. The earth upon it showed dark through patches of heather, and it was as red as if the blood of warriors had been spilled upon the ground.

At the foot of the hill the giant woman built her

smithy, and placed her anvil within it. She built a fire of birchwood beside the anvil, adding fuel and blowing upon it with her bellows until the flame leaped high and the heart of the fire, like the sun at midday, glowed too brightly for the eye to look upon.

She cast red earth from the hill on the fire and melted it, and worked it into a fiery ball. Taking the ball with her tongs she laid it on the anvil, and with her hammer she beat it with all her might, and her arm moved so swiftly it seemed that the smith had seven hands. She shaped the glowing metal into a blade, and as she worked she murmured to it, whispering magic runes, until the blade took form and leaped on the anvil and sang back to her, and so the sword was born.

The Finne, in the pursuit of Lon Lonnrach, the giant woman, met and passed a bard of their clan. He was curious to know what game they tracked so hotly, so he turned about and followed after them.

While the sword was yet in the making the Finne came to the smithy and stood peering through the narrow slit that served for a door, watching the gruagach at her work. As the blade on the anvil took shape beneath her hammer, Finn, impatient to see the weapon closer, put a hand on either side of the doorway and tore the opening wider. He passed into the smithy and went to stand at the bean-gruagach's side. And after him came Osein, Coilte, Diarmid, Osgar the son of Osein, and Goll Mac-Morna, and presently the bard of the clan, having found his way to them at last, came in to join them.

The gruagach, until the shining blade was finished,

paid the intruders no heed. Then she laid the sword aside and set the hammer against the anvil on the ground. She turned to Finn and a smile full of evil and malice showed on her face. "Since you came unbidden, Finn Mac-Chumhail, you are unwelcome," said she. "Better for you 'twould be, if you had stayed behind."

Finn had eyes for naught but the sword. His heart leaped for joy at the sight of the gleaming weapon.

"Whether I be welcome or not is of little consequence," he said. "Strike a bargain with me, O uallach gobhain, to whom the smithy's mysteries are known. What will you take for this blade of earth and fire, and for others like it, one for each of my chiefs who are with me here?"

"The earth's wealth, the sea's wealth would not purchase even one sword were I in Lochlan," said Lon Lonnrach the bean-gruagach. "But I am in a strange land and far from my home. What do you offer me for the swords?"

"For each sword I will give ten golden chains, each the length of the sword, and golden armlets and wristlets enough to cover each sword from end to end," said Finn.

With a screech of scornful laughter the giant woman replied, "I see your lips move, and your mouth seems to form words, but no sound do I hear. You must speak louder—and to better purpose, Finn MacChumhail!"

"Let us have done with the haggling!" Finn shouted. "Waste no time in idle talk. Tell me what price you set upon the blades!"

"For each sword you must give me one hundred golden

chains, and one hundred wristlets, one hundred armlets, one hundred finger rings, all of ruddy gold."

The chiefs at Finn's side stirred uneasily and protested.

"Six hundred chains, six hundred wristlets, six hundred armlets!" exclaimed Osein.

"And beside, six hundred rings," Diarmid added.

" 'Tis a hard bargain you drive, Lon Lonnrach," said Goll MacMorna, frowning.

"Take it or not, as you please," the gruagach said.

But Finn spoke up, silencing the others. "You shall have the price you demand," he told Lon Lonnrach. "Make us the swords."

Six were the days of the forging of the swords, counting the day on which the first one was made, until the day upon which the last blow of the hammer was given to the last blade on the anvil. The fire glowed hotly, the red earth turned to a molten ball in the leaping flames, the hammer beat out its song, and a sword was finished and laid by with the others beside the anvil, day by day. Early in the morn of the fifth day, Finn sent Goll Mac-Morna home to fetch the price of the swords. Toward midday of the sixth day, Goll, returning, approached the smithy with the gold chains and armlets, the wristlets and rings, in a great sack on his back.

When he was coming through the glen that led to the smithy he met the bard of the clan who had come to meet him.

"There's trouble in store, Goll MacMorna," the bard said. "Set down your burden and hear what I have to say."

Goll was not unwilling, since his load was heavy, and he had walked far with it that day. He lowered the sack to the ground and sat down beside it, and waited for the bard to speak again.

"From the day my eyes first beheld Lon Lonnrach I have mistrusted her and doubted her goodwill toward the Finne," the bard told Goll MacMorna. "She is a creature of deceit and lies, as foul within as she is hideous to see. In the long years of my life I have learned of some of the ways of magic, and among them the power to read the thoughts of others. Deep and dark is the mind of Lon Lonnrach, and full of wickedness. But she has not been able to hide from me the plan she has made to destroy Finn and his chiefs."

"What can she do against us?" scoffed Goll MacMorna. "There being six of us, and each man of us nearly as big as herself."

"By wiles and witchcraft," said the bard.

"Have you not warned Finn and the others, that they may be on their guard?" asked Goll.

"Warned them? Have I not tried!" cried the bard. "They are all too bemused and enchanted by the beauty of the blades, the like of which they have not seen before in all their days. They are like men in a trance! When I speak they will not listen. Finn says, 'Leave me! I will talk to you another day.' Coilte and Osgar and Osein bid me, 'Be off!' and as for Diarmid, he shakes his head as if I were a gadfly buzzing around it, and says nothing at all."

"Aye," said Goll MacMorna. "I see how it is. Well,

then, since there is no one else who will listen to you, you may as well tell me."

"This gruagach keeps in her mind the secret of the forging of battle weapons. She is the guardian of the uallach gobhain, the mysteries of the smithy, and calls herself by that name. One of the secrets in her mind concerns the tempering of the swords she makes. No sword beaten out upon her anvil will ever be battle-worthy unless it is bathed in blood before it is ten days old."

"Hoo!" grunted Goll MacMorna, beginning to understand.

"Aye!" said the bard. "What the miserable ugly creature has in her mind is to give the swords their first taste of blood by plunging them into the hearts of Finn and his chiefs. She has not forgotten you, Goll MacMorna. You will be counted with the dead—if she succeeds."

"Life is sweet to me, O bard my kinsman," said Goll. "I am too young to yield it willingly. But what of Finn and the others? Here we sit, wasting the precious moments, and there is no telling what may be happening to them."

"They are safe for the time," the bard told him. "She has thrown dust in their eyes, which has put them into a deep sleep. It is for you she waits, Goll MacMorna, and the treasure you bring to pay for the swords. She will not harm them until she is sure of the gold. But having laid hold of that, her plan is to get rid of you first. The others, lost in their slumbers, will be at her mercy then."

"So it is with my blood she means to temper the first sword!" said Goll MacMorna. "I am not sure her choice has been wise." His mouth set grimly. "There seems to be an even chance. She dies or I do. Well," he said, as he rose and shouldered the sack of gold. "Perhaps I will be able to tip the balance my way."

Into the smithy came Goll MacMorna, bearing the sack of golden chains and armlets, wristlets and rings, upon his shoulder. He saw Osein, Coilte, Diarmid, Osgar the son of Osein, and the fair Finn himself, lying deep in slumber against the farther wall. The bean-gruagach turned from the forge and her one eye glistened as she beheld the sack of gold. "Welcome!" she said, speaking fair words in a soft voice. "You came in good time. Here is the last of the six swords—just ready, Goll MacMorna, for you." She came forward, the sword in her outstretched hand. "Do you see anything that needs to be done yet?" she asked as, smiling horribly, she approached him.

"That I will have to see for myself!" said Goll Mac-Morna. He dropped the heavy sack from his shoulder with a sudden jerk that sent it thumping down upon the woman's toes. "Aie! My toes! My toes!" she cried. "My toes are broken! Broken! Broken!" She forgot the sword and her intention to temper it in Goll MacMorna's blood. She thought only of the pain that she felt, and stooped to rub her aching toes.

Goll MacMorna snatched the sword from the hand of Lon Lonnrach. "There is just one thing it needs!" he said, and he plunged in into the gruagach's treacherous heart. With an air of satisfaction Goll MacMorna looked at the blade as he drew it out. "This sword is well-tempered," he told the bard. "I will have this one for my own."

When Finn and his chiefs were roused from the sleep that was caused by the magic dust, each man took a sword for himself and tempered it in Lon Lonnrach's blood. Then Finn turned to his chiefs. "I am a great fool," said Finn MacChumhail. "I am a fool of fools, to trust a bean-gruagach, and one from the land of Lochlan beside, and put you all in peril of your lives!"

"The guilt is equally ours," said Osein.

"Did we hold you back?" asked Coilte.

"The business did not end badly," said Diarmid.

"No harm was done to anyone of us," said Osgar son of Osein.

"And the swords," said Goll MacMorna, "are ours. And the treasure as well."

Then the Finne made a bier of branches. They put the body of Lon Lonnrach, the hideous, treacherous, evil bean-gruagach upon the bier. They carried her over the brown hill, and over the green hill, and over the yellow hill and across the plain. They came to the shore and cast the body of Lon Lonnrach into the sea. There the waves took her and carried her back across the sea to Lochlan and cast her up on the shore from which she came. On the shore of Lochlan the Yellow Muilearteach, the father of Lon Lonnrach, waited for his daughter to come home with the swords and the stolen treasure. Her body was washed up at his feet. He saw the six wounds, made by the six swords Lon Lonnrach had forged in the land of the Finne. He shrieked wildly, and shook his fists and stamped his feet with rage, but all his fury could not bring the giant woman back to life again.

There was a great feasting in the land of the Finne, to honor Goll MacMorna, who had slain the bean-gruagach and saved the lives of Finn and his chiefs. The bard who followed them to the red hill made a new song about the adventure. He called the song *"Duan na Ceardach"* ("The Lay of the Smithy"), and it was sung for the first time at Goll MacMorna's feast.

At the time of the feast, each chief took his sword in his hand and gave it a name by which it would hence-forth be known. These are the names of the six swords made by Lon Lonnrach the bean-gruagach, as set down by the bard in "The Lay of the Smithy":

Of Osgar son of Osein
    Druidhe Lannach (Magic Blade)
Of Coilte
    Chruaidh Cosgarreach (Hardy Slayer)
Of Diarmid
    Liobhanach (The Polisher)
Of Osein
    Ceard nan gallan (The Tinker of Striplings)
Of Goll MacMorna
    Fasdail (Make Sure)
Of Finn MacChumhail
    Mac an Luine (Son of the Surge)

While the bard of the clan was reading the thoughts of Lon Lonnrach, he read also (and reading, learned and remembered) all the mysteries of the smithy that she had hidden there. The secret lore, the bard taught to men who used it for the good of the Finne.

Then there were blacksmiths throughout the land as there had never been before. The tunnachen, the fire-hardened poles and staves, were cast aside forever. Every warrior had his battle weapons, his dagger, his sword, and his spear, made according to the mysteries of the smithy, the uallach gobhain, by the mating of fire and red earth, beaten out by the hammer on the anvil in the same fashion that Lon Lonnrach had forged the six swords for Finn and his chiefs.

The Tale of the
Lay of the Amadhain Mhor

IN the olden times long before our days there dwelt in Caledonia a fearless warrior who was of great renown throughout the land. Hosts fled from him in battle and no man could withstand his might. Far and wide, he was known as the Amadhain Mhor, the Great Fool, because he relied not upon his sword and his spear, but in combat would throw away his weapons and trust to the grasp and the strength of his own two arms. He had never felt defeat nor known the meaning of fear. Many great chiefs were subdued by him and many a knee was bent to pay him homage, and at last no one dared to challenge his rule.

Then said the Amadhain Mhor, "There is no one left to stand against me. Shall the sinews of my good arm wither

for lack of use? I shall sail over the sea to Lochlan and seek a worthy opponent there."

In his tall-masted ship with the black sails the Amadhain Mhor set forth to Lochlan. He took no servants, no page to wait upon his needs. His one companion was his young wife, Gealmhin, the delicate fair one, whom he loved well.

The strong hands of the sea waves took hold of the ship and urged it forward. The breath of the wild wind filled the tall black sails. Wind and waves speeded the ship to Lochlan and carried it up on the shore. The Amadhain Mhor left his ship beached upon the strand and with his fair young wife he went up from the shore to travel into the land.

In those days the land of Lochlan was the dwelling place of wizards and witches. Magic spells were laid to trap the unwary voyager, and giants peopled the place.

The Amadhain Mhor and Gealmhin had not gone far beyond the sea when they came to the edge of a lovely glen. Soft grew the grass underfoot, roses flourished abundantly, the leaves of the trees stirred in the breeze, and waterfalls played gentle music for the ears' delight.

"We will go into this glen," said the Amadhain Mhor. "I am weary of seafaring and need to rest."

"O Amadhain Mhor, my loved one," said Gealmhin. "Go not into the glen, I beg of you. My heart tells me that evil lurks beneath the beauty there."

"He who is strong need fear no evil," said the Amadhain Mhor. "Come with me and I will protect you, my delicate fair one. Or, if you fear too much, stay here and wait for my return."

"Nay, where you go, I shall go," said the young Gealmhin. "But alas, you are only too truly called the Amadhain Mhor. Foolhardy man, who waits not for danger to come to him, but plunges into it headfirst!"

"Let us go into the glen," said the Amadhain Mhor.

They went into the glen and the grass was cool under their feet, the breeze refreshed them, and flowers scented the air about them. But when they were well within the glen, with half of its length behind them, a great fog rose about them and shut the glen and its beauties from their eyes. From all sides there came rough winds to buffet them. They heard strange noises, voices wailing and skreighing, loud bursts of thunder, and the rush and roar of hidden waters. Fog swirled about them in gray circles until they grew dizzy and sank down upon the ground.

Then, through the fog, they saw one coming toward them. Half-hidden in a misty cloud, a giant approached, bearing in his hands a great jeweled cup.

"Now, when my thirst is greatest, help arrives!" cried the Amadhain Mhor. "Come then, gruagach! Let me drink from your cup."

"Nay!" said Gealmhin. "Touch not the cup the stranger offers! Drink not, nor eat, within the borders of this enchanted glen. There is naught but mischief in all things here."

"Foolish youth! Do you refuse the cup that will refresh you?" asked the giant, laughing. "Farewell to you, then. I shall go on my way now." And he turned to leave them.

"You shall not leave until I have slaked my thirst," cried the Amadhain Mhor, and reaching out, he seized the cup and quickly drained it to the last drop.

A draught of misfortune that was indeed for the Amadhain Mhor! The cup he drank from held a magic potion. No sooner had he swallowed the draught than his legs vanished from the knees down to the soles of his feet.

"O my Amadhain Mhor, my Great Fool," wept the fair Gealmhin. "Ah, that my warning found your ears deaf. Who, now, in all the world will fear to fight you, and you but half a man without your legs?"

"I will walk on my shanks, then, and fight on them, too, if I must. And I will go after this giant of the cup. He shall not be rid of me until I have my legs again," said the Amadhain Mhor. Then up he got and stumped along through the glen, walking on his knees, following the giant of the jeweled cup. But the giant sped before him, and soon was hidden in the fog.

"Let us go no farther lest worse befall us," pleaded Gealmhin. "Let us return to the ship and sail back to our own land."

"I shall get my legs back first," said the Amadhain Mhor, "or there will be no man in all the world who will have two legs to walk on."

They came to the end of the glen and found themselves upon a wide stretch of moorland upon which the sun shone brightly. The sound of hunting came from the wood that grew at the end of the glen. Presently a stag came racing out of the wood and over the moor. The Amadhain Mhor seized his throwing spear and cast it at the deer as it sped by. The spear pierced the stag through its two sides and it fell dead. Then a fine great staghound, white-coated and red-eared, wearing a golden collar, came baying out of the wood in pursuit of the deer. The Amadhain Mhor reached out and caught it by its golden collar as it raced toward him. He wove a leash of strong young hazel withes and looped it through the staghound's collar. He gave the leash to Gealmhin, and bade her hold it fast.

"Stay here and sing to me," the Amadhain Mhor told the white staghound, "till one comes from the hunt for you."

Out of the wood came a giant huntsman. So handsome a man the Amadhain Mhor had never seen before. The giant walked in splendor, wearing a cloak and a helmet of the purest gold. His hand rested on the golden hilt of a sword that hung at his left side. On his right arm he bore a golden shield and in his right hand he carried a golden crossbow and two throwing spears.

The sun's rays, glancing from the gold cloak and helmet, surrounded the handsome giant with shafts of golden shining light. He came striding down from the glen and halted beside the Amadhain Mhor.

"My stag that you have slain and my hound that you have caught are mine by right," said the giant in the cloak of gold. "I have come to claim them, and send the hound back to the chase."

"Never again shall you boast that you are the master of

the great white staghound," said the Amadhain Mhor. "The hound remains with me. As for the deer I have slain, I shall keep that, too."

"If you will not give up the hound and the stag of your own free will, then you will have to fight for them," the golden giant said. "In all the days of my life, I have never been defeated, and it is not my intention that you will beat me now."

"In all the days of my life," replied the Amadhain Mhor, "I have fought no fight that I have not won. You are the master of the hunt and you have hounds galore. This one you can easily spare. But though I am a poor lamester, I do not fear you. All I have is the stag I have slain and the hound I have caught, and to keep them I will fight you, if that is your desire."

Then strength against strength, they threw themselves into the struggle, wrestling back and forth across the moor. The earth was rocked by their strife, rocks bounded from their places and trees bowed down. But when the battle was done, the golden giant lay defeated. The Amadhain Mhor was the victor, and he had won the right to keep the white staghound and the deer. The golden giant rose from the ground and said to the Amadhain Mhor, "The white staghound is yours, and the deer to you, also! My heart is downcast, for the hound is dear to me, and I have never tasted defeat before. But I am not ill-pleased that I was beaten by an opponent as worthy as yourself, who despite the lack of his two legs had the courage to strive against me. Let us be foes no longer, but clasp hands in friendship. You and your fair wife shall come with me to my house and be my guests. Food, clothing, and shelter shall be provided for you there, and all other things you desire."

Said Gealmhin, the delicate fair one, "This giant shows a noble spirit in his defeat. Can you do less, O Amadhain Mhor? I beg of you, let him have back the hound. You will miss it less than he, who loves it well."

Then said the Amadhain Mhor, "Your wisdom, Gealmhin, is greater than my own. Would I not have my two legs now, if I had heeded your warning in the glen? Since it is your wish, he shall have back the white staghound."

The three went on together. In the hollow of his shield the giant carried Gealmhin, the delicate fair one, and over his shoulders, the stag, while the white-coated, red-eared staghound paced between his master and the Amadhain Mhor.

The moor rose to a hill and at the top they looked down upon a pleasant valley. At the side of the vale there stood a citadel of gold. Every spire and turret and tower sent shafts of shining light upward toward the sun.

"What is this place of wonders?" cried the Amadhain Mhor. "Who dwells within its walls?"

"This is the City of Gold," said the giant. "It is my house, and within its walls there dwells no men of guile, but only myself and my beautiful wife.

"You must see my wife to understand how great her beauty is," said the golden giant. "Her skin is like the snow at its first falling, her mouth a rose lying on the snow. Her eyes are twin lakes reflecting the blue of the heavens, and in her heart dwells innocence itself. Each day, while hunting, I go through the glen of enchantment. It is full of glamour, and witches in the guise of fair women beckon to me and seek to entice me. All their wiles are useless and only make me value more my beautiful young wife."

They came down to the City of Gold, and a lady blessed with great beauty, the wife of the golden giant, came forth to greet her husband and welcome his guests. "Who is this fair lady?" she asked. "And who is the big man you have brought to our house?"

"This is the Amadhain Mhor," said her husband. "And this lady is Gealmhin, the delicate fair one, who is his wife. All the men of the world are at the beck and call of this great warrior, and I myself among the rest."

"You tell me a wonderful thing!" said the beautiful lady. "But if the men of the world are at his command, how was it that he let his legs go with them?"

"O wife, I give you my word," said the giant. "The men of the world are indeed at his beck and call. And legs or no legs, I, who have never before known defeat, have myself been vanquished by his might! If he had not met with witchcraft in the enchanted glen, his legs would not be gone. But come! The Amadhain Mhor and I have clasped hands and are foes no longer, and he and fair Gealmhin are friends in my house."

"It is enough," said the beautiful lady. "If they are your friends, they are mine also." She smiled upon them sweetly, and kindly led them into the house. She brought food to them and drink, and bade them refresh themselves, and rest.

"There is no match in all the world for this lady's beauty!" said the Amadhain Mhor.

"Her beauty is greater because it goes hand-in-hand with kindness," replied Gealmhin, the delicate fair one, who, though young, was wise.

Then spoke the golden giant. "Now I shall return to my hunting, to the moorland and the enchanted glen. Remain here, O Amadhain Mhor, my friend, to watch over my house, my wife, and my treasure of gold. While I am out, I lay it upon you to let no man enter, but if, by chance, one should come in, see to it that he does not go out again!"

"I give to you my promise that it shall be done as you say," said the Amadhain Mhor.

The golden giant went off to the chase, taking with him his white staghound. The beautiful lady settled herself in her tall golden chair by the window to wait for her husband's return, while the Amadhain Mhor and Gealmhin, the delicate fair one, rested on a cushioned bench by the fire.

"O Gealmhin," said the Amadhain Mhor. "The mists of the enchanted glen have not yet cleared away from my eyes. My head is heavy. I will lie down for a minute or two and rest."

He put his head down in her lap and at once fell asleep. While he slumbered a tall brown giant came in from the road and gave a kiss to the golden giant's wife. The beautiful lady made no protest, but smiled, and lowering her eyes, sat quietly in her tall golden chair.

Fair Gealmhin beheld the giant come in and leaned to

her husband's ear. "Wake up! O Amadhain Mhor," said she. "Unlucky your sleep has been. A warrior in brown came in and kissed the golden giant's wife."

The Amadhain Mhor sprang up from the bench and set himself at the door. He struck the posts on either side a blow with his mighty fists. And never a stronger blow was struck by a blacksmith, tinker, or wright than the blows of the Amadhain Mhor. He took his stand and blocked the door and none could pass by him. "Easy it was, O giant in brown, to come in while I slept," said he. "But you will find it a harder thing to get out again, now I am wide awake."

The giant seized the Amadhain Mhor to haul him out of the way. "You have not the right and you have not the might to keep me in," said he. "Move out of the doorway, nor stand in my path when I want to go out!" he cried.

But still the Amadhain Mhor stood firm, like a boulder at the door, and all the brown giant's strength could not prevail to move him out of the way.

"Give up the struggle. I fear you not, and your strength is no match for mine," cried out the Amadhain Mhor. "And you shall stay in until he who is out comes back to his City of Gold. And when he comes he'll pay you well for the kiss you gave his wife."

Then the giant in brown, seeing that his strength was useless against the might of the Amadhain Mhor, sought to beguile him.

"Mighty one," said the brown giant. "I see your wisdom is as great as your strength. I will give you seven chests full of shining gold. I'll give you cattle in herds and good free land, and a castle of your own. You shall have all that, and more, for I will give you my finest cloak, my swiftest hound, and my horse who goes as well on the sea as he does on the land. All these I shall give you, if you will move aside and let me go out."

"Save your breath and keep your wealth," said the Amadhain Mhor. "All these things are of no value against the promise I made to the giant of the City of Gold. All your riches would not console me if my honor were lost. You shall stay in, and when the giant comes he'll pay you well for the kiss you gave his wife."

"As I came through the glen of enchantment," the brown giant told him, "I met with the giant of the jeweled cup who tricked you out of your legs. He let me have one of your legs lest I needed to bargain with you. I will blow your leg back in place under you, if you will let me out."

"I'll take the leg and set it in place with my own magic," said the Amadhain Mhor, and seizing the leg from the giant's hand, he set it beneath him where it belonged.

"You have the leg I offered," the brown giant said. "It is time now for me to depart."

"Stay where you are for a little longer," said the Amadhain Mhor. "I made no bargain with you, but took the leg from you and put it in place myself. Furthermore, my other leg is needed before I walk like other men. If you got one leg from the trickster who stole them, no doubt you got the second. I will have both my legs from you or you will go without your head!"

Then "Help!" and "Mercy!" cried the brown giant as the Amadhain Mhor lunged toward him, driving him before him, until the giant took refuge behind the beautiful lady's chair. "Save me from this Amadhain Mhor!" the brown giant cried. But the lady smiled, and bowed her head and said nothing at all, sitting quietly in her tall golden chair.

"Ho, then!" said the Amadhain Mhor. "If death be a terror to you, hand me over my second leg, or before I can say 'snipp, snapp!' your head will roll about your feet!"

The brown giant gave up the other leg and the Amadhain Mhor set it beside the first one in its right place. "My two good legs are mine again, and I can walk as other men," rejoiced the Amadhain Mhor.

"It is time now for me to depart," said the brown giant with his eye to the door.

The Amadhain Mhor took his stand in the doorway again. "You shall stay in," said he. "The day will not come when you will go out, till comes the giant of the City of Gold."

"Oh! Ho!" said the brown giant, laughing, as he threw aside his brown helmet and cloak. "It is I myself who am the giant of the City of Gold! And I am also the giant of the jeweled cup who took away your legs. And I am the brown giant who came in while you slept and kissed the beautiful lady, my wife. Each disguise was assumed that I might test your courage and your honor. O Amadhain Mhor, your renown has been for your might before, but now it shall be for your courage and faithfulness as well.

28 .

We shall be as brothers henceforward, and you and your wife, Gealmhin, the delicate fair one, shall dwell with me and my wife, the lady blest with beauty, forever in the City of Gold."

Then the beautiful wife of the golden giant stepped down from her tall golden chair.

"Was it not right that my husband should give me a kiss when he came in?" she said, smiling. "But, then, he could not disguise himself from me."

Then all four clasped hands, gave love for love, and goodwill for goodwill, and ever after lived together like the fellowship of the Finne.

S dh'imich an sgeul mar sin.

(And so passeth the old tale away.)

The Tale of the
Lochmaben Harper

THERE was an old harper of Lochmaben town, and he played his harp and played it well, with a

> Dum ti tiddely,
> Um ti diddely,
> Daddely, diddely,
> Dee dum do!

His harping brought him such fame that folks from far and near came trooping to hear the tunes of the Lochmaben harper. He'd give them a sad and a sorry song that would make the tears spring to the eye, then in a trice he'd strike up a tune so blithe and gay that heads would be nodding and feet would be tapping, and folks would be laughing and shouting with glee, before their

tears had time to dry. Och, aye, a merry old body was he, the harper of Lochmaben town, with his

> Dum ti tiddely,
> Um ti diddely,
> Daddely, diddely,
> Dee dum do!

This merry harper took a great delight in a wager or a bet. Many a guinea of gold was laid by the lairds and the lords of Lochmaben town against the harper's one wee crown. His luck was aye in, for he ne'er lost a stake and whate'er the wager, he'd win it. The lairds would lower and grumble, and swear the de'il himself was in it! But the de'il had naught to do with his winning, because, to tell you true, the harper was sharper than the lairds. So he'd pocket their gold and off he'd go, with his

> Dum ti tiddely,
> Um ti diddely,
> Daddely, diddely,
> Dee dum do!

King Henry of England in London town sat drinking his cup of wine. "'Tis time," he said to his chamberlain, "for a royal progress through our domain." So he summoned his lords of high degree, his nobles and his knights, and bade them all ride out with him to keep him company. And with him he took his huntsmen bold, his horses and his hounds. And with them, led by a trusty groom, was that steed of great renown, King Henry's favorite, Wanton Brown.

The king's domain was long and wide. For days, through the English countryside, the company rode, mile after mile, and the lairds and nobles and knights would fain have found themselves at home again. The roads were miry, the weather was wet and chill, the day was dark and dreary, the lords and nobles and knights and all were saddlesore and weary. They begged the king to stop a while and rest in his castle in Carlisle.

"I' faith," quoth the king. " 'Tis what we'll do! We'll hold court here for a fortnight—or maybe two."

Then the company, one and all, found comfort and cheer in the castle hall, while in the stables, in a warm stall, the groom put that steed of great renown, King Henry's favorite, Wanton Brown.

Two Scottish lairds were riding along the road that led to Lochmaben town when whom should they meet but the merry old Lochmaben harper, with his

> Dum ti tiddely,
> Um ti diddely,
> Daddely, diddely,
> Dee dum do!

They stopped to pass the time of day. Then said Sir John, "Now have you heard the Sassenach king is biding a while at the castle of Carlisle?"

"Aye," said Sir Charles. "And he's brought a sluagh of lordlings and callants along wi' him, too."

"Och, havers! Your news is new no more. I've heard the tale you tell before. But do ye ken that they've brought that steed of great renown, King Henry's very favorite, Wanton Brown?" asked the Lochmaben harper.

"Och," sighed Sir John. " 'Tis a noble beast. And worth his weight in gold, at the least. I've ne'er laid eyes upon him myself."

"Nor I," said Sir Charles. "But I'm telling you true. 'Tis what I would like to do."

"So I would, too," said Sir John.

"I would not have you want, my lairds," said the sly old Lochmaben harper. "So over the Border to England I'll slip and steal the horse and then, when you have had a good blink at him, you may take him back again!"

"You're daft!" cried Sir John. "You cannot do it."

"You silly loon!" said Sir Charles. "Och, you'd be caught, and the king would hang you on the spot!"

"What will you wager against a crown that I will not go to Carlisle and bring King Henry's Wanton Brown here to Lochmaben town?" asked the canny old Lochmaben harper.

"Five acres of good plowed land," said Sir John. "If you come home alive to tell the tale."

"I'll wager five thousand pounds in gold," said Sir Charles. "And a safer bet was never made."

"The wager is laid," the harper said. "Five acres and five thousand pounds against my crown that I will fetch, for you to see, King Henry's Wanton Brown."

The Lochmaben harper went home to his wife. "I'm off to Carlisle," said he, "to steal King Henry's Wanton Brown for the Lochmaben lairds to see."

"Then take along the old gray mare that yestreen had a foal," said she. "Take the old gray mare, but leave the foal at home with me. Hide a halter under your cloak till you can steal the Wanton away, then slip the halter over the steed's nose and tie the lead to the tail of the gray. Then let the old gray mare go free, and off she'll speed, like a hiving bee, to her foal that's here at home with me. She'll never stop for food nor drink till she comes to Lochmaben town. And willy-nilly, tied to her tail, she'll bring King Henry's Wanton Brown!"

"Praise God who gave me a wife with wits!" said the harper. "I'll do as you say." So with his harp, on the gray mare's back, he merrily rode away, with his

> Dum ti tiddely,
> Um ti diddely,
> Daddely, diddely,
> Dee dum do!

The Lochmaben harper came to Carlisle and went harping through the town. Hard by Carlisle Castle gate he met a man coming down, with jeweled coat, and feathered cap, and many a golden chain and ring. When the harper asked folk who he was, they said 'twas Henry the English king.

"Light down! Light down!" King Henry said. "Old harper, your music I must hear!"

"Oh, by my sooth," the harper said. "I cannot play till I find stabling for my gray mare."

"Go down below to the outer court that stands by the town. You'll find room there to stable your mare beside my good steed Wanton Brown."

The harper went to the outer court and found the

stable there. Beside King Henry's Wanton Brown he tied up his old gray mare.

With his harp on his arm to the gate he went, and into the castle hall, to harp for King Henry, his lords and his knights, his huntsmen and nobles all, with his

> Dum ti tiddely,
> Um ti diddely,
> Daddely, diddely,
> Dee dum do!

The harper played and the harper carped and the king and his lordlings swore that never in all their lives had they heard music so sweet before. So still they stood a body'd have thought they were rooted to the floor, and even the grooms crept in to hear, and forgot to lock the stable door.

The harper harped and the harper carped a lay so soft and slow that the king and his lords all nodded their heads and off to sleep did go. One by one they closed their eyes and lay in slumber deep. The harper looked them over and laughed to see that every soul was asleep.

Then quickly he slipped off his shoon and softly crept down the stair to the outer court below, near the town, to see how matters stood there.

There was never a body in sight, and the stable door was standing wide. Finding a lantern to give him light, the harper quietly stole inside.

Five and thirty horses stood, stamping their feet and champing their food. Three and thirty the harper passed without a glance till he came at last to his old gray mare by that steed of great renown, King Henry's favorite, Wanton Brown.

He took the halter from under his cloak and set the lantern out of the way. The halter he slipped o'er the nose of the brown and tied it fast to the tail of the gray.

Then he led the mare to a small back gate that opened out on the town, and step for step as she trotted along came King Henry's favorite, Wanton Brown. He set the mare free with a thump on her rump. "Be off, auld lass!" cried he. And like an arrow shot from a bow, off at a gallop went she. Down the road, and over the bridge, and in and out of the town the gray mare sped, and close behind galloped the Wanton Brown.

When the noise of their hoofs was heard no more the harper slipped back to the castle hall and, bent o'er his harp, he went to sleep with the king, his nobles, and knights, and all.

The old gray mare was swift of foot and she tarried for naught along the way. To the harper's door in Lochmaben town she brought herself and the Wanton Brown at the breaking of the day.

"Lass, get up!" called the harper's wife. "And help your master stable the mare."

The serving lass peeped out the door and saw the two horses standing there.

"Mistress," she cried. "The master's not come, but a wonderful sight to see! The gray mare's had another foal, and it's bigger by far than she!"

"Och, ye silly wench!" said the harper's wife. "It's daft wi' sleep you be! Come ben the house and go back to bed. I'll get up and go myself to put the mare in the shed."

The harper's wife clapped her hands for joy and chuckled at the sight of the old gray mare and Wanton Brown in the early morning light. "Get in to your foal," she said to the mare. "You've done a good job this night."

She loosed the lead from the gray mare's tail and foddered and bedded the two of them down. Then she locked the shed that none might know that it held that steed of great renown, King Henry's Wanton Brown.

The groom woke up in the castle hall early in the morn. To the stable he went where the horses stood, stamping their feet and champing their corn. Three and thirty horses there were where five and thirty there should be. The groom gave a blink at the empty stall and cried out, "Woe is me!" He hurried back to the castle hall on legs that shook with fear, and shouted like one whose wits are gone, "King Henry's Wanton Brown's awa', and so is the silly old harper's mare!"

The harper feigned to weep and lament. "Och, a wretched body I am! The English loons have stolen my mare, and she with a newborn foal at home that'll die without its dam!"

"If there be rogues in Carlisle town, I've suffered for it too," said the king. "They've stolen my Wanton Brown, so I've lost a horse as well as you."

Said the harper, "My loss is twice as great!" and he cursed and tore his hair. "You've lost one horse but I have lost two, for I'll lose the foal as well as the mare."

"Hold your tongue!" King Henry said. "You'll have no

cause to lament and swear. I'll give you thirty guineas to pay for your foal, and three times thirty to pay for your mare!"

Little did King Henry know 'twas the harper who'd stolen his Wanton Brown. The king put the gold in the harper's hand and the harper went harping from the town, with his

> Dum ti tiddely,
> Um ti diddely,
> Daddely, diddely,
> Dee dum do!

Sir Charles and Sir John rode out again and they looked over dale and down. They saw the harper come over the hill, a-harping into Lochmaben town. They caught up with him on the road. Said Sir John, "Are ye back so soon?"

"I thought you went to Carlisle," said Sir Charles, "to steal the English king's steed, ye loon."

"I doubt ye've won the wager," said they. "Come, pay us over your crown."

Said the harper, "To England I have been and harped for the king in Carlisle town. The music I made he liked so well that he gave me a bag of gold, and it as full of guineas bright as ever it would hold." He took a long white bag from his pouch and jingled it merrily. "I've brought back a bag of gold," he said, "and the Wanton Brown for you to see."

"You lie!" said Sir Charles.

"You lie!" said Sir John. "The steed is guarded by night

and day. 'Twould take a craftier thief than you to steal the Wanton Brown away!"

"Your words are harsh," the harper said. "But I will gladly pay over my crown if, when you come to my stable with me, I do not show you that steed of great renown, King Henry's favorite, Wanton Brown."

To the harper's stable the two lairds went, and he opened the door and there, plain to be seen, was the Wanton Brown beside the harper's old gray mare.

"I've kept my word," the harper said, and a merry man was he. "I've brought King Henry's Wanton Brown, my lairds, for you to see."

The harper had won the wager again, and the two lairds had to pay. Sir John made over the land he'd staked, and Sir Charles paid up five thousand pounds, ere the dawn of another day.

They swore that never again would they lay a wager against the harper's crown. Then back to the English king they took that steed of great renown, King Henry's favorite, Wanton Brown.

Long in Lochmaben the harper did dwell with his wife and his mare and his land and his gold, and now there's no more of the tale to be told, but he played his harp and played it well, with a

> Dum ti tiddely,
> Um ti diddely,
> Daddely, diddely,
> Dee dum do!

The Tale of the
Earl of Mar's Daughter

HAPPEN you've heard many a tale about one Earl
of Mar or another. Surely their names have been known
through the ages for deeds of daring, but there is a story
about the daughter of one Earl of Mar that is better than
all the others put together.

The green summer is bonnie, and once, on a pleasant
summer's morn, this noble Earl of Mar's daughter ran out
of her father's castle to sport and play with her maids in
the dewy fresh morning air. The sun rose high and
bright, and the day grew warm, so they threw themselves
down to rest from their play in the cool shade of a green
oak tree. The Earl of Mar's daughter looked here and
there about her, to see what she could see. She saw the
green grass and the flowers in bloom and the little white

clouds in the bright blue sky. And she saw a bonnie white turtledove preening his wings as he sat at the top of a high stone tower. A bonnier bird she had never seen, and the sight of him so delighted her eye that she raised her voice to call him down and coaxed him to fly to her hand.

"My bonnie bird, O my Coo-me-doo," she cried. "Come down to me, come down! You shall have a cage made of good red gold instead of a nest of straws, beneath the eaves. I'll put golden curtains to your cage and silver hangings on the wall. Of all the birds in Scotland you shall be fairest of all. I will tend you with care, and love and cherish you, my Coo-me-doo, if you will come down to me."

No sooner was the promise made than the dove came flying down. He lit on her shoulder and folded his wings as if contented to stay. The Earl of Mar's daughter laughed for joy to find the dove was won. She carried him back to the castle that morn and made him a place in her bower. Her promise she kept, for she gave him a cage all made of the good red gold. She fashioned it all so fair and fine, with silver hangings and curtains of gold, that never a bird in all the world was as gay as her bonnie dove, Coo-me-doo.

The day was passing and night was nigh, and it was eventide. The Earl of Mar's daughter sat in her bower with only her bonnie turtledove to keep her company.

She sat in the dusk with the bird on her wrist, and smoothed his feathers down, then all of a sudden he slipped away from under her hand, and was gone. She looked to see where he had flown, and not a sign of the bird did she see. But, standing beside the golden cage, she saw a strange handsome young man.

The lady jumped to her feet in alarm. "From whence have you come?" she cried. "I bolted the door of my bower myself. What way have you found to come in?"

"Earl's daughter, hush you!" he said and smiled. "So foolish you cannot be! Have you forgotten your bonnie white dove that you brought home today?"

Then she looked high and she looked low, but there was no bird to be seen. There was naught but the empty golden cage and the strange handsome young man.

"Oh, tell me who you are, young man!" the Earl of Mar's daughter cried. "And what have you done with my bonnie dove, my Coo-me-doo?"

"I am your bonnie dove, your Coo-me-doo," the smiling stranger replied. "My mother dwells far, far away on an island in the sea. Wealthy she is, beyond believing, and noble and powerful, too, for she is the queen of all the foreign isles. In magic, too, she is skilled, and she has laid spells upon me so that I become a dove all the livelong day, until night falls, when I become the man you see. This she has done that I might beguile young maidens like yourself. This morning I first came from my mother's isle, over the stormy sea, with her spells newly laid upon me, and yours was the first maiden's face that took my eye. You have so charmed me that I have no wish to look farther, and if you consent, I will remain with you forever, my dear love."

Then said the Earl of Mar's daughter, "Oh, Coo-me-doo, my beloved, never again shall we be parted. You shall stay with me, night and day, until we die."

"Then the spell upon me which makes me bird by day and man by night must ever be a secret," said Coo-me-doo. "If it became known my death would surely follow, for by day I cannot protect myself."

"I will keep the secret," the Earl of Mar's daughter said. "No one shall learn it from me."

Then the two lovers plighted their troth, clasping hands, and became man and wife.

Seven years the Earl of Mar's daughter and her Coo-me-doo lived happily together and each of the seven years brought them a young son. Each of these seven years Coo-me-doo, as soon as the child was born, carried it over the sea to the foreign isles and left it in his mother's care, lest its presence betray the secret they had hidden so well.

But, when seven years more had passed by, there came a great laird to the castle of the Earl of Mar. He saw the earl's lovely daughter sitting by the window of her bower with her white dove, Coo-me-doo, perched upon her hand.

She was so fair to see that he wanted her for his wife, so he came courting, bringing her costly presents to win her favor. Her father, the Earl of Mar, thought well of this fine suitor and bade his daughter accept him, and be his wife.

" 'Tis high time that you were wed," said the earl. "The years are getting on and you are not getting younger. 'Tis unlikely you'll have another offer half so good. The man is a laird, with great estates and with wealth galore. What more can you ask to wed?"

But the Earl of Mar's daughter refused. She returned all the presents the great laird sent her and told her father she would not wed him, nor any other man.

"I'm contented as I am," said she. "I ask no more than to be left to live alone, with only my bonnie dove, Coo-me-doo."

Then her father, sitting among his nobles in his castle hall, shouted loud in his anger. "In the morn before I break my fast or slake my thirst, I'll have the life of that cursed bird Coo-me-doo! I'll wring the neck of my daughter's dove in the morning and marry her to the laird at noon!"

"Coo-me-doo, my love so true," the Earl of Mar's daughter said. "Spread your wings quickly and fly away to save your life. I must remain here, but I will die before I wed the laird or any other man."

Then said Coo-me-doo, "Aye, my true love, I must no longer stay with you, lest we both be forlorn. Wait here, my beloved, in your father's hall, and do not lose hope, though hope seem vain. To my mother I'll fly for help across the sea to the island where I was born. When morning comes my neck will be far away from your father's angry hands."

Away he flew, and long that night the Earl of Mar's daughter wept, and her tears fell fast as she sat beside her white dove's empty cage.

Far over the stormy sea the bonnie white dove flew, until he came to the island where his mother dwelt. He flew to his mother's castle and lighted there upon the top of a high golden tower. His mother came walking out and looked about to see what she could see, and she saw her son, the bonnie white dove, sitting high on the golden tower.

"Get dancers for dancing!" the queen cried with joy. "Get harpers for harping! Let us be merry, for here's my young son come home to see me this day."

"Nay, mother, get no dancers for dancing and get no harpers for harping," the white dove replied. "For my love, the mother of my seven sons, is being forced by her father to marry a great laird and tomorrow is her wedding day."

"Oh, tell me, tell me," his mother cried. "Tell me true and tell me quickly, what I must do for you?"

"Instead of dancers for dancing," said Coo-me-doo, "instead of harpers for harping, take four-and-twenty good stalwart men and turn them into great storks with feathers of gray. Turn my seven sons into seven great swans to fly above them, and myself into a gay goshawk to lead them all."

Then the queen, his mother, said, "That is a thing too great for my magic." But she bade her son not to despair. "I know an auld-wife who dwells nearby whose skill is far greater than mine," she said.

The auld-wife was brought and brewed her bree and cast her spells. Her magic was mighty indeed. Instead of dancers for dancing and harpers for harping, there were four-and-twenty stalwart men turned into storks with feathers gray. The seven sons were seven great swans to fly above them high, and Coo-me-doo was a gay goshawk ready to snatch his prey.

They rose up together in a flock and flew across the stormy sea, and came to the Earl of Mar's castle, and there they perched on the trees near the gate at noon on the wedding day.

The folks that came to the wedding looked up, amazed to see so big a flock of great birds, such as they had never seen before.

The wedding train came from the castle, and the Earl of Mar's daughter came first, on her father's arm. Her maidens came walking along behind her, and then the bridegroom, with his best man at his side. And after them all, the wedding guests came dancing at the end of the line.

Down the road to the kirkyard they went, but before they reached the door of the kirk, the great flock of birds flew out of the trees and swooped down upon them all.

The great gray storks seized all the wedding guests so that they could neither fight nor run away, while the seven swans tied the Earl of Mar, and the bridegroom, and his best man fast to the trunk of a great oak tree. The swans took hold of the bridesmaids and the gay goshawk caught up the bride. Then up rose all those great pretty birds into the air, and in the blinking of an eye, birds, bride, and bridesmaids were out of sight.

There are old, old men still living who have been heard to say that they've been at weddings these sixty years or more, but in all their lives they have never, before or since, beheld so strange a wedding day.

There was nothing the folk there could do and nothing they could say, when the flock of great bonnie birds came down and carried the bride and her maids away.

When they flew back across the sea, the queen of the isles cried out with joy, "Get us dancers for dancing! Get us harpers for harping! Let us be merry, for here is my son and his wife come home to stay with me!"

After a while the Earl of Mar's daughter sent word to her father to tell him where he could find her, and being at heart a sensible man, and lonely beside, he forgave her. So now the Earl of Mar and his daughter, they visit back and forth, which is well, for thus the tale ends happily.

The Tale of
Dick o' the Cow

ALL the Armstrongs were reivers and robbers in the old days, and there was a mighty lot of them dwelling in Scotland along the Scottish Border. There were so many of them that folk said that if a fighting force should ever be needed, they would be able to muster five thousand well-armed men. One and all, they had a remarkable taste for high living and a noble distaste for honest toil, so they avoided working for the luxury they loved and managed to get it by going a-raiding along both sides of the Border, lifting the beasts and the gear of their neighbors, and carrying away whatever they could lay their hands upon. Anyone who lived within riding distance they looked upon as a neighbor, and they never minded going twenty miles or more in the darkness of the

night, providing the booty they got from their unwilling hosts made the journey worthwhile. They were always impartial in their choice of victims, and raided the dwellers along both sides of the Border. Scot or Sassenach—'twas all the same to them.

These Armstrongs had grown so powerful and daring that the very mention of their name scared most folk out of their wits, but there was one man got the better of them once, and that was a poor innocent called Dick o' the Cow. And him an Englishman, too!

Dick o' the Cow did not come by his name because of any cattle. In Scotland beasts of that sort are known as kine. Dick got his name because the house he lived in was so thickly set about with cow, or broom, that it was hard to tell whether it was a house at all, or only part of a big bushy clump. But for all that, it was a good wee house with two rooms to it, one of which housed Dick and his goodwife, while the one at the back was where Dick kept his three fine milk-kine.

Dick's house stood on the estate of the Laird of Hutton Hall, and Dick was in service to the laird. But Dick was not only a worker on the land. Although he was generally known as an innocent, as Scots call one whose wits are a little bit lacking, still Dick was something of a wag, and mad and merry beside, so the Laird of Hutton Hall employed him as his fool. And it was this poor silly fool that got the best of two of the worst reivers that ever belonged to the Armstrong clan.

The Armstrongs had a great liking for the name of John, so much so that half of the men of the clan bore

John for their given name. To avoid confusion when so many had been christened John Armstrong, it was the custom to tack some sort of description to the name, and there were rafts of nicknames such as Lang Jock, Wee Johnnie, Cruikback John, Red John, Black John, Brown John, Muckle-mou' Jock, and many more.

One of these John Armstrongs was the Laird's Jock, so called because his father was Simon Armstrong, the Laird of Mangerton, and it was the two sons of the Laird's Jock—his eldest, another John Armstrong, known as Fair Johnnie, and his youngest son, Wullie—that Dick o' the Cow paid off in their own coin.

Some folk said the Laird's Jock was better than the general run of Armstrongs, or maybe they only said he was no worse than the rest. But nobody had a good word for Fair Johnnie, who was a big yellow-haired laddie with a quick temper and a ferocious grin that struck terror to the heart of anyone who saw it. As for young Wullie, he was a feckless lad without much gumption, so he usually followed along wherever Fair Johnnie led.

The raids of the autumn had paid the Armstrongs so well that they were able to lie in during the winter weather without troubling themselves with new supplies for the larder. But when spring came on, some of the men began to fret against the long do-less days.

Fair Johnnie said to his brother, young Wullie, "Och, we've lain at home o'erlong. Our horses are growing fat and lazy, standing idle in their stalls. A-riding and a-reiving we'll go, to let folk know we're still alive!"

So over the Border they rode that night, with their

minds on Hutton Hall some twenty miles away. It was well known that the Laird of Hutton Hall was proud of his fine milk-kine. His herds and his flocks were said to be the best in all Cumberland.

Fair Johnnie and Wullie came over the hill and looked down to Hutton Hall. The moonlight shone down on empty fields where only six old sheep strayed, cropping the grass on the lea. There were no herds of fine fat kine grazing there at all. The Armstrongs sat in their saddles and cursed till the air about them grew blue. They'd made the long trip in vain, for the canny Laird of Hutton Hall was too cunning for those two lads. His gear was all stored and his beasts were all penned behind good strong stone walls.

"Six sheep is better than naught," said Wullie, but Fair Johnnie shook his head.

"Let the six old sheep graze on, for all of me," said he. "Rather than drive these auld crowbait wethers twenty miles home to Liddesdale, I'd leave my body dead here in Cumberland."

So Wullie shrugged his shoulders and waited to find out what Fair Johnnie meant to do.

"Hey, Wullie!" said Johnnie suddenly. "Who was that poor silly man we met t'other side of the hill? The one that pointed us out the way to Hutton Hall?"

"Och," said Wullie. " 'Twas naught but the fool of Hutton Hall's laird, the innocent that folk call Dick o' the Cow."

"Dick o' the Cow!" Fair Johnnie said. "I thought it must be he. They say the fellow has three fine milk-kine that he got from the Laird of Hutton Hall."

He grinned at Wullie and Wullie grinned back, with the same thought shared by those two. They turned and rode back down the hill till they came to the house of Dick o' the Cow.

Dick and his goodwife were fast asleep and the reivers let them be. On the points of their toes they made their way till they came to the end of the house. They peeked in through the window hole, and there in the straw below they saw the three big fat milk-kine that Dick had got from the Laird of Hutton Hall.

"Whether I live or die," Fair Johnnie said, "those three milk-kine are going to Liddesdale this night with me."

So stealthily did the two thieves work that scarcely a sound was heard in the stillness of the night. But they broke the house wall open wide, and through the gap they took the three fine kine of Dick o' the Cow.

As they started on their homeward way, driving the kine before, Wullie stopped his brother and said, "The kine are good and make it worth coming so far. But we need a bit of gear beside, to make the value more."

So Wullie went through the gap in the wall again, and crept around and about in the house, and he stole three coverlets off the bed where Dick and his wife were lying asleep.

When morning came, Dick's wife arose, and saw the hole in the wall. She soon discovered the kine were gone, and her three coverlets as well. She shouted and cried and wrung her hands, and wildly ran about.

But Dick cried out. "Wife, hauld your tongue! From your weeping let me be. I'll go, and for each cow you've lost, I swear that I'll bring you back the worth of three!"

He knew where his kine had gone and who had taken them away, for had he not met with Fair Johnnie Armstrong and young Wullie, his brother, over the hill the night before?

So Dick went off to Hutton Hall to tell his sad tale to his master there, but his master thought it was one of Dick's foolish jokes and paid him little heed.

"Be off with you, Dick!" said the laird. "I have no time for your jests this morn."

"I've no time for jesting myself," said Dick. "And what I tell you is true. The Liddesdale Armstrongs were in my house last night, and they've stolen away my three fine kine, and three coverlets off my bed."

"That's very bad, and very sad," said the laird. "But what would you have me do?"

"I can no longer in Cumberland stay to be your fool and your loyal man," said Dick. "So, master, give me leave to go to Liddesdale and steal."

"Give you leave to steal!" cried the laird. "That, by my honor, I cannot do, unless you vow on your solemn oath to steal from none but those men who stole from you."

"I give you my promise," said Dick o' the Cow. "And I swear by my troth to you that I will not steal so much as a straw from any but those who stole from me!"

Then Dick o' the Cow took leave of the laird, and went and bade his wife farewell. As he went through the town he bought a good bridle and a pair of new spurs and packed them into the leg of his breeks and started for Liddesdale.

The Laird's Jock kept his house at Tenisborne, and in the Laird's Jock's house were Fair Johnnie, his young brother, Wullie, and a score and ten of the Armstrong kin. Dick came to the Laird's Jock's house and looked about him on every side. Here and there, indoors and out, he saw Armstrongs galore.

"Wow! Here am I, one innocent fool," said Dick to himself. "And the Armstrongs number thirty-and-three!"

But he stepped inside the house and went straight to the chair where the Laird's Jock sat.

"Well may ye be, good Laird's Jock," he said, "and well may ye ever be. But the de'il himself may fly away with all your company. Last night Fair Johnnie, that limmer o' hell, and his brother Wullie, too, they broke into my house and stole away my three good kine and three of my goodwife's coverlets."

Fair Johnnie jumped to his feet in a rage. "Hang the fool," cried he. "Fetch me a good strong rope, for I swear he'll not go out of Liddesdale alive!"

"Nay," said Wullie, "to hang the fool would be a troublesome job. Slip a wee dirk between his ribs. That way 'twill be easier far."

"Hauld, now!" cried Geordie's John, one of the kin. "Why kill him, poor silly man? Toss him in a four-corner-ed sheet, and then beat him well and let him go home."

"While this is my house," the Laird's Jock said, "we'll have no hanging or slayer or beating here!" And he stared them down with an angry eye. "Sit ye down, man," he said to Dick, "and when the food's ready, you shall have some of your own kye."

But Dick drew back to a nook by the fire when the dinner was set down. He wanted no food, for he knew well he never could stomach the meat of his stolen cow.

In the house of the Laird's Jock there was a rule that those who came late for the meal should have none at all, but must bide their time until the next mealtime came around. That made those lads who were last to come in hastier than they should have been for fear they might be forced to fast till meat was put out again. Dick from his corner by the fire saw that the ones who came in last, in their hurry not to be late, instead of hanging the key to the stable door on its hook, tossed it up on the ledge above the door. Dick took good notice with both his eyes, for he meant to make use of what he saw.

Dick curled up in his nook by the fire, and feigned to be asleep. He snorted and snored like a boiling pot, but he watched the Armstrongs all the while. They guzzled their stolen beef and their ale until they could hold no more, then every man of them settled himself, to sleep before the fire.

When Dick was sure they were all asleep, he got up and crept to the door. He took the key from the place where it lay, and out of the house he slipped. Into the stable yard he went, and opened the door with the key. Thirty-three horses were in the stalls, but Dick had an eye for only three. Thirty belonged to the Armstrong kin, and those thirty Dick tied with Saint Mary's knot which means that he cut the hamstrings of every horse and left them crippled behind in their stalls. Then he let loose the other three. He took them into the stableyard where the

moon shone bright, to let him see that he had Fair Johnnie's, young Wullie's, and the Laird's Jock's horses, all
three. Dick took out the bridle and spurs that he'd tucked
away safely in the leg of his breeks. He put the spurs
upon himself and the bridle on Wullie's steed, then he
leaped on Fair Johnnie's horse and tickled its sides with
his spurs.

The spurs were new and the spurs were sharp, and
Fair Johnnie's horse reared when he felt their steel. Away
he dashed at a good round pace, as if the de'il were at his
tail, and Wullie's horse was close by its side, for Dick
held fast to its bridle rein. But Dick left the horse of the
Laird's Jock behind, loose in the stable yard, for the Armstrongs to see that Dick could have taken him too if he
liked, but he would not steal from the Laird's Jock, who
had stolen naught from him.

Fair Johnnie rose in the early morn and went out to the
stable to feed his horse, but the creature was not there.
His brother Wullie's was gone as well, and his kinsmen's
were crippled, every one, and the only horse left of thirty-
three was the one that belonged to the Laird's Jock.

Fair Johnnie ran back into the house and woke his
father up. "Wake up, Laird's Jock!" he cried. "That silly
fool, Dick o' the Cow, has gone off with Wullie's horse
and mine. There's thirty tied with Saint Mary's knot, and
your own is the only one left that a man can ride."

"You ne'er would be told!" the Laird's Jock said. "Now,
did I not tell you true when I said to keep out of Cumberland or trouble would come to you?"

"Who would have thought that an innocent could be

as canny as he?" said Fair Johnnie. "Och, come now, Laird's Jock, will you not lend me your horse, that I may go into Cumberland and fetch my own horse and Wullie's home?"

The Laird's Jock said, "No!" and he said, "No!" and he said, "No!" again, but Fair Johnnie would not hold his tongue until the Laird's Jock agreed. So the Laird's Jock lent Fair Johnnie his horse, and arms and armor beside— a coat of mail, and a steel head-cape, and a two-handed sword, and a spear.

Fair Johnnie put the armor on and took his sword and his spear, and away he galloped on the Laird's Jock's horse in pursuit of Dick o' the Cow. He caught up with Dick on Carnaby Lea, and Dick turned and stood his ground. Fair Johnnie hurled his spear at Dick, but it missed and went to the side, and it did no harm but to cut a slit in the skirt of the jerkin Dick wore. Fair Johnnie took up his two-handed sword and rode at Dick with a frightful yell.

"No swordsman am I," said Dick o' the Cow, "but I have a sword myself." So then Dick drew his own sword out, and waited for Johnnie to come by, and more by luck than by any skill, he dinged Fair Johnnie a blow on the brow with the pommel of his sword. The blow put Fair Johnnie in a daze and all his wits were gone. He pitched over the head of the Laird's Jock's horse and lay as if dreaming on the ground.

Dick saw that he'd be sleeping a while. Said he, "I've won the battle this day. And from all I've heard, it's not stealing at all to carry the spoils of battle away. And

though this is the Laird's Jock's gear, and his horse, 'tis
Fair Johnnie who has them now, so I'm not stealing from
the Laird's Jock at all, when I take my spoils from Fair
Johnnie, his son."

When Dick rode away from Carnaby Lea, a doughty
man was he, for he was clad in the jacket of mail and in
the steel head-cape, too. He bore away the two-handed
sword, and his own, and Fair Johnnie's spear as well.
Fair Johnnie's horse he rode again, but he led at his side
young Wullie's horse and the one that Fair Johnnie had
borrowed from the Laird's Jock.

When Fair Johnnie woke up on Carnaby Lea, a dreary
man was he. Up he got and limped off home, and he
swore as he went that never again, if he lived to be a
hundred years, would he fight a fool, after what had
happened to him that day.

Dick rode straight to Hutton Hall to show his master
what he had brought home. When the laird saw the
booty he'd taken, he shouted angrily that he'd take care
that Dick was hanged for all his thievery. Dick's feelings
were sorely hurt at his words. "My laird," said he, "you
know well I'd never have gone into Liddesdale to steal
without your permission to go. By the bargain you made
with me I had the right to go and steal from those who
had stolen from me."

"I gave you that leave indeed," said the laird. "But
what made you steal from the Laird's Jock? His horse, his
sword, and his jacket and head-cape and all?"

"I swear by my troth I've stolen naught from any man
who has not stolen from me. The armor and the horse I

took were the spoils of battle, you see, and I took them after I'd bested Fair Johnnie in a battle on Carnaby Lea. And if they were once the Laird's Jock's gear, it was from Fair Johnnie I won them away."

"Since you have kept your word so well, I'll say no more," said the Laird of Hutton Hall. "And I'll tell you what I'll do. I'll take the Laird's Jock's horse off your hands, since you'll not be needing three."

"Nay," said Dick. "I'll not be needing three."

"I'll give you one of my best milk-kine," said the laird. "And I'll give you twenty pounds beside, for the Laird's Jock's horse."

"My laird, I may be a fool," said Dick, "but a bigger fool you'll not make of me. You must give me the cow and *thirty* pounds, or I'll sell the horse at Mattan Fair."

Dick set his price and would not change, so his master had to pay. And Dick went off with a fine milk-kye, and thirty pounds that he got for the horse.

When Dick went out of Hutton Hall's gate, whom should he meet coming in but the Bailiff of Glozzen-berrie, who was brother of Dick's master, the Laird of Hutton Hall.

"Where did you get Fair Johnnie's horse?" asked the bailiff. "I know the creature well, for I've seen Fair Johnnie astride its back very often, at Carlisle."

Then Dick told the bailiff all the tale of how he went to Liddesdale and came home with booty enough to pay for his three stolen cows, that the Armstrongs had carried away.

The bailiff laughed till his sides were sore. "For a fool,

you are wondrous wise!" said he. "And I'll tell you what *I* will do. I will buy Fair Johnnie's horse for the same price that my brother paid for the one he bought."

"A man with one horse has no need of two," said Dick o' the Cow. "He can ride but one at a time. If you will pay what my master paid, then you may have Fair Johnnie's horse."

The bailiff gave Dick a fine milk-kye and put thirty pounds in his hand, and Dick handed over Fair Johnnie's horse and started off for his home. When Dick o' the Cow came into the house, his wife began to lament and wail.

"Now hauld your tongue, goodwife!" said he. "And from your crying leave me be! You shall no longer complain, for you have no cause that I can see. I've brought you two kine and either one is as good as all three that were stolen away, and here are sixty good pounds to pay for your three coverlets. And beside all this, there's a suit of armor, a sword and a spear, and Wullie Armstrong's horse for me."

The very next day Dick o' the Cow went to the Laird of Hutton Hall, and a sorry man was he. "I may no longer in Cumberland dwell, to be your fool," said he. "The Armstrongs, they live too near to this place, and I fear they'll catch me and hang me high."

So Dick o' the Cow and his goodwife packed up their gear and flitted away. They went to Burgh under Stanimuir, and as there were no Armstrongs near, they may be living there to this day.

The Tale of
Bonnie Baby Livingston

NO one could ever hope to see a bonnier lass than Bonnie Baby Livingston. There wasn't a soul in the whole of Dundee who would not have said that she was the fairest lass in all the town. She had such sweet and winning ways that the other lasses didn't mind if she outshone them—at least not very much. And as for the lads, whenever she walked out to take the air, they came tumbling and trailing after her, like puppy dogs at her heels.

Among the throng who followed in her train there was a wild young Highland chief, the Laird of Glenlion by name. He was a big, handsome young fellow, inclined to bluster and brag a bit, and anybody could see at a glance that he thought uncommonly well of himself. When he

strutted along the streets of Dundee with his Highland bonnet atilt on the side of his head, wearing a gay tartan plaidie folded over his shoulder, you couldn't miss seeing the jaunty lad. With his green velvet jacket, his fine white linen shirt with a lace frill down the front of it, and his kilt swinging to and fro in time to his swaggering stride, he was a sight to be seen. And just to add to the elegance of his costume, his sword was hung at his side and his dirk was tucked into the top of his stocking. When he passed by folk turned to gape after him, then they grinned and said, "Och, aye! The Laird o' Glenlion's loose again!"

It was this fine gentleman who set his heart on winning Bonnie Baby Livingston for his wife. But Baby had no notion of what was in the young laird's mind. If it had ever occurred to her, she'd have laughed at the thought of becoming the bride of Glenlion. She had been bred to the gentler manners and quieter dress of the town, and she found his wild Highland ways too rough and rude to suit her taste. Although he had good looks, a title, a castle, and money galore, he had no chance at all of winning her heart. She had already given that to a fine young man of Dundee named Johnnie Hay, and Johnnie had given her his to make it a fair exchange.

At first Glenlion could not bring himself to believe that her love could not be won by him. But when he found out that it was true, his pride was sorely wounded to find himself so disdained by the lady he'd chosen to wed. If he had been able to get so much as a smile or a kindly look from her, at least he could have hoped. But though he waited and sighed and followed her about for months on end, de'il a bit of a smile or a look of kindness did he get in all that time to ease his pride or his heart. When at last he stopped to consider the time he had spent trying to win her favor, and all of it wasted, it was too much for his hot Highland blood. The worst of it was that the lass did not just snub him. She overlooked him, as if she did not know he was there. Whenever he came near her, she looked straight by him, as if she did not see him, and away she'd sweep on the arm of Johnnie Hay.

As might have been expected, there came a day when the Laird of Glenlion decided that he had had enough of being slighted. It was beyond bearing, he told himself, and he was the man to put a stop to the silly lass's nonsense. "Whether she will or no," he vowed to himself, "Bonnie Baby Livingston is going to be my wife!"

By some strange trick of fate, that was the very day when Baby slipped away from her friends and walked out of the town by herself to watch the country folk making hay. And along the road on his tall black steed, the Laird of Glenlion came. To his joy and surprise, who did he see walking along before him but Bonnie Baby Livingston, all by herself alone.

He spurred up his horse and dashed to her side and swept her up into his arms. Before she could catch her breath or call for help, he had set her before him on his steed and galloped off at top speed. Alas for Bonnie Baby Livingston! The Laird of Glenlion had stolen her away.

He took away her silken coat and he took away her satin gown, and he rolled her up in his tartan plaid, and wrapped her closely round and round. In the curve of his arm he held her tight and she could not move nor turn. He would not let her speak a word, nor look back at the road by which they came. The black horse sped along like the wind over hill and dale and down, till they came to a Highland glen, where they met with Glenlion's brother Jock with twenty armed men.

"Come, brother, turn back," Glenlion said. "Tomorrow will be my wedding day, and you must stand as my best man when this bonnie lady and I are wed."

Then Jock turned his horse about, and back he rode at Glenlion's side, and ten armed men before them rode and ten armed men behind.

They came through the glen to the top of a hill where Glenlion stopped, and bade Baby look down. There was a wide green brae below with many cows and sheep.

"There's a hundred cows grazing there, and a hundred ewes beside," he said. "And they all belong to me."

But Baby was so weighed down with woe that she would not turn her head around to look down the wide green brae.

Then Glenlion bent down and kissed her cheek. "I'll give you all these cows and all these ewes, and more beside," said he, "for only a single kindly look or a smile from your bonnie blue eyes."

"You may keep all your cows and all your ewes for yourself," said Bonnie Baby Livingston. "And you'll get no kindly look and no smile from my eyes unless you take me home again and set me down safe in Dundee."

"Dundee, Baby? Dundee, Baby?" Glenlion said, with a

laugh of scorn. "Dundee you'll never see, till I've carried you to Glenlion castle and you are wedded to me. We'll bide a bit at Auchingour to sup on sweet milk and cheese, then off to Glenlion castle we'll ride, where you shall become my bonnie bride."

"I will not stop at Auchingour!" cried Baby. "I want no milk or cheese. To Glenlion I will not go, and I will never be your bride!"

"Whether you will or no," said the laird, "you will do as I say. The mistress of Glenlion castle you'll be, and tomorrow will be our wedding day."

Then Glenlion's brother Jock spoke up. "I tell you, brother, if I were you, I'd take that lady home again, for all her bonnie face. Better a lass that's loving and kind, though maybe not a lady born, than one whose heart you have not won, for she'll make your days heavy with hatred and scorn."

"Och, hold your tongue now, Jock!" said the laird. "You do not know what you say. My heart has been lost to that bonnie face for a good twelvemonth and more. I've loved her long, and I've loved her true, and I've sworn my wife she'll be. And now that I have her in my grasp, I'll never let her get away."

"Have your own way," said his brother Jock. "But I doubt it will bring you much joy." And having had his say, he wasted no more words, but silently rode on at the Laird of Glenlion's side.

They came to the end of their journeying as day was closing in, and saw the castle's gray walls and towers against the evening sky. Glenlion's three young sisters came out to welcome the travelers home. They put their arms around Baby's waist and led her gently into the hall, and each sister gave her a greeting warm, but she did not reply. She stood among them silently, and said no word at all. They unwrapped her from the plaid and brought her a dress of their own to wear. They bathed the salt tears from her face, and gently smoothed and combed her hair. They set her at the head of the table, and plied her with food and wine, but still she sat silent, not heeding them, and would not eat or drink.

"Take her away and let her rest," said the laird. "The lass is too travel-worn to eat. She'll be hungry enough tomorrow, when she sits at our wedding feast."

So the three young sisters took Bonnie Baby Livingston to a bower in one of the towers, and bidding her lie down and sleep, they left her there alone. When they had gone she ran to the door and opened it, but there were men standing at the foot of the stairs, so she could not go that way. She ran to the window, but the ground was too far below to leap out, and the wall too steep to climb down, and there was no other way by which she might escape. She sat down in a chair by the window, and leaned her head on her hand and wept.

While she sat there weeping the door opened softly and in slipped the laird's youngest sister, Jean. She saw Baby sitting there wrapped in grief, and crossed the room to her side.

"Oh, lady, do not weep," said Jean, "and do not look so sorrowful. Tell your trouble to me and maybe it will ease your sad heart."

"Why should I tell my trouble to you?" said Baby. "I have no friends in this strange place."

"Then take me for your friend," said Jean. "I promise that I will help you if I can."

"Your brother, the Laird of Glenlion, has stolen me away from my family and all my friends, and from my true love in Dundee. Oh, if I but had pen and ink and paper, and someone to carry the letter I'd write, I'd send it to me true love. There might be time for him to come and rescue me."

"I will help you," said Jean, "if you will swear to me that my brother will never know. Heaven knows what he would do to me if he found out."

Then Jean brought paper, pen, and ink, and a candle so that Baby could see to write a letter to her true love, Johnnie Hay.

Then Jean went away again and came back with a young Highland laddie whom she had secretly brought into the tower. He was a bonnie lad in his philabeg and bonnet, and Jean had chosen him because he was both fleet of foot and strong.

"This lady," Jean told him, "has an errand for you to go."

"If you would win my blessing this night," said Bonnie Baby Livingston, "carry this letter to Johnnie Hay at Dundee. Bid him make haste to come and rescue me." Then she showed the laddie a golden chain, and three golden guineas beside, and promised he should have them all if his errand was well-sped.

No lad in the Highlands could run so swiftly. He ran

over hill and dale as fast as a bird could fly. As the hour of midnight struck, he came to the town of Dundee, and knocked loud and long at Johnnie Hay's door. Johnnie rose up in alarm and threw open his window and cried out, "Who's there?"

"I've brought you a letter from your lady," said the laddie. "If you want to save her, you'll have to come down quickly and speed back to Glenlion with me."

When Johnnie read the letter, an angry man was he! He swore that before the morning broke, the Laird of Glenlion would give up Bonnie Baby Livingston, and if any harm had come to her, the Highland laird would sorely rue this day.

He cried to his grooms, "Come saddle the gray horse for this braw laddie. And saddle for me my milk-white steed, for it is the fleetest that ever rode out of Dundee. He sent word to all his kinsmen for them to come out to join him, and they came riding, one hundred strong.

"Arm yourselves well and follow me," cried Johnnie Hay. "We're off to Glenlion castle, for the Laird of Glenlion has stolen my true love away. I swear I'll neither eat nor sleep until Bonnie Baby Livingston is safe at home in Dundee!"

Then Johnnie mounted his milk-white steed and put the laddie on the gray, and with his kinsmen he galloped off, and reached Glenlion in sight of the castle walls about the break of day. They left their horses on the road and through the gates crept quietly. Johnnie's kinsmen took places to guard the door, but the laddie took Johnnie to the wall below the window in the tower.

At the window Baby stood, as the morning mists were rising gray, and she heard her true love calling to her and looked down, and there below was Johnnie Hay!

"Jump from the window, Baby!" he said. "You need not fear to fall. My arms are strong to hold you safe, and my kinsmen are at the castle gate, so you're free from Glenlion's power."

But Baby feared to leap so far, for the tower window was high, so she made a rope of her coverlets and tied it fast above, and then she climbed down along the wall and Johnnie caught her in his arms before her foot could touch the ground. Then he set her before him on his horse and the two of them merrily rode away. As they sped away Baby looked back at the castle and cried with glee, "Glenlion, you have lost your bride. She's gone off with her true love, Johnnie Hay!"

Glenlion sat with his brother Jock, waiting for the priest to come. As Johnnie and Baby rode by the gate, the young laird heard the ringing of Johnnie's bridle chain. The laird called out to his brother Jock. "Go meet the priest and bring him in! I hear the clang of his bridle chain." Well pleased he was, as he laughed and said, "Now Bonnie Baby Livingston will be my wife before the larks rise up to sing."

Jock looked out the grill of the door, and back to his brother he ran and said, "Brother, that was no priest who came, and if he comes now, he'll come too late. There's a hundred of Johnnie Hay's kinsmen, armed with swords, standing outside at the castle door."

The Laird of Glenlion stood in his hall, and raised a

shout for his men. "Arm yourselves!" cried the Highland laird. "And take your swords in hand. We'll make these Dundee rascals sorry they came here today!"

Glenlion's men all drew their swords and gave a warlike shout. But with a hundred of Johnnie Hay's men outside to stand against the laird's twenty men, not one of Glenlion's men dared to be the first one to go out. So there they stood with their swords in hand, all the livelong day, while Bonnie Baby Livingston rode safely home to Dundee with Johnnie Hay.

The Highland laddie was a wise chiel. He rode behind them on the gray, and when he got to Dundee he took service with Johnnie Hay. Then Baby gave him the golden chain, and the three bright guineas of gold, and Johnnie gave him twenty pounds for running his errand so well that night. But he never went back to Glenlion again, for he thought it wiser to stay away.

Glenlion and his brother Jock and all their twenty armed men were shut up in their castle till night fell again. Then Johnnie's hundred kinsmen went marching home to Dundee, singing all the way:

"Away, Glenlion! Away for shame!
Go hide yourself in your glen!
You've let your bride be stolen away,
For all your armed men."

The Tale of
Lang Johnnie Mor

DID you hear the tale of young Lang Johnnie Mor, the braw big laddie from Rhynie at the foot of Benachie? Johnnie was a good-sized lad for his age, which had just turned twenty years. It took three yards of leather belt to gird his waist around, and his shoulders were two yards wide. Lang Johnnie Mor was sturdy and strong, and the sword at his side was ten feet long, and Johnnie himself was fourteen feet in height.

Johnnie was not a man to waste words, so when he went away from Rhynie at the foot of Benachie he did not trouble himself to tell his kin and his friends where he was going or why. But news has a way of traveling till it gets to the place where it belongs, and folks in Rhynie found out what had become of their Lang Johnnie Mor.

Said one to another, "If all be true they tell, and I suppose it be, it's off to Lunnon town young Lang Johnnie Mor has gone."

"Och, aye," said t'other. "And if all be true I hear, and I suppose it be, he's gone to carry the banner there, for the Sassenach king."

Then everybody said that, being a Rhynie lad, young Johnnie Mor would do well, no doubt, and now that they knew where Johnnie was, they went about on their own affairs.

When Johnnie had dwelt in Lunnon town for a twelve-month and two, or maybe three, the fairest lady in the town fell in love with the bonnie big lad. She smiled so sweetly on Lang Johnnie Mor whenever he passed by, that what could young Johnnie do but fall in love with the fairest lady in Lunnon town?

Had his lady been a serving lass, or Johnnie a noble of high degree, the lovers would never have found a cloud to cast a shade on their joy. But the lass young Johnnie took for his love was the king's own daughter, and Johnnie was naught but the lad who carried the banner for the king.

The news ran all around Lunnon town till it reached the ear of the king that his banner bearer, Lang Johnnie Mor, and his noble daughter had fallen in love. The king, he reared and shouted with rage, and swore it should never be. He took his daughter and carried her up to a room in a high stone tower, and he locked the door and pocketed the key.

"Stay there and starve, fair lady," he said, "for you'll get no meat or drink from me."

Then down he went, and angrily vowed that before the week went by, the weighty young Scot should stretch a rope, for he would be hanged on the gibbet tree. Lang Johnnie Mor paid little heed when they told him what the king had said. "They must catch me first," said he. "While I have my good sword in my hand, no man will dare lay a finger on me."

But the English king was cunning and sly. He found three rogues and paid them well to steal into the house where Johnnie dwelt and put poppy-seed oil in Johnnie's ale. Johnnie came home and drank his ale and sleep overpowered him soon. He fell to the floor and there he lay, like a man in a swoon. Then the king sent his soldiers in, and they fettered young Johnnie where he lay. When he woke he was sorely amazed to find that his hands were bound with iron bands, and his legs weighted down with a hundredweight of chains.

"Where will I find a wee little lad who will work for me?" young Johnnie cried. "Where will I find a wee little lad who will work for me and carry a message to Auld Johnnie Mor, my uncle, at Rhynie at the foot of Benachie?"

There was a wee little lad by Johnnie's door, and he spoke up. "Here am I, a wee little lad," said he. "And I will run on, to take a message to Auld Johnnie Mor, your uncle, at the foot of Benachie."

"You will earn your meat and your fee," said Lang

Johnnie Mor. "Run on, my wee little lad. When you come to the brae where the grass grows green, throw off your shoes and speed away. And when you come where the streams run strong, bend your bow and leap over, or swim! When you come to Rhynie you'll not need to call or seek about the town. You'll know my uncle, Auld Johnnie, there, for he stands three feet above them all."

Then Johnnie said to the wee little lad, "Bid my uncle make haste lest they hang me high, and bid him bring along with him that stalwart body, Jock o' Noth."

The wee little lad set his feet to the north, and on his errand he sped away. When he came to the brae where the grass grew green, he cast his shoes aside and ran on. When he came to the streams that flowed fast and deep, he bent his bow and leaped over or swam. And when he came to Rhynie at last, he had no need to go seeking through the town, or to call. He knew Auld Johnnie at first glance, for he stood three feet above them all.

"What news?" Auld Johnnie asked. "What news, my wee little lad? I've never seen you here in Rhynie before."

"I bring you no news," said the wee little lad. "But a message I bring to you, from your nephew, Lang Johnnie Mor. The king has put young Johnnie in chains, and he threatens to hang him high. Johnnie bids you haste to his aid, and to bring with you that stalwart body, Jock o' Noth."

Benachie lies low in the dale, and the top of the Noth is high, but Jock o' Noth on his mountaintop heard every word of Auld Johnnie's call.

"Come down! Come down! O Jock o' Noth, come down in haste to me. My nephew, Lang Johnnie, needs us sore, so we must go to Lunnon town."

Then Jock o' Noth came down from the hill and met with Auld Johnnie at the foot of Benachie, and these two mighty men together were an awesome grisly pair to see. Their heads peered down through the boughs of the trees, and their brows were three feet wide, and there was no less than three good yards across their shoulder bones.

These two great bodies started forth. They ran o'er hill, they ran o'er dale, they ran o'er mountain high, and they came to the walls of Lunnon town at dawning of the third day. When they got there the city gates, with iron bars and iron bolts, were closed and all locked tight, and on a tower a trumpeter stood with his trumpet in his hand, ready to blow it and give the sign for Lang Johnnie Mor to be hanged. The keeper of the gates looked out to see who knocked so loud outside. Auld Johnnie asked, "What goes on inside that the drums beat with a mournful sound and church bells toll so solemnly?"

"There's naught that goes on," the gatekeeper said. "And naught that matters to you! Just a weighty Scot to straighten a rope, for Lang Johnnie Mor will be hanged today."

"Open the gates!" Auld Johnnie cried. "Open the gates without delay!"

The gatekeeper trembled, but grinned and said, "Kind sirs, I do not have the key."

"You'll open the gates," Auld Johnnie said. "You'll open

them without delay, or here's a body at my back who will open them for me!"

"Open the gates!" roared Jock o' Noth, "or I'll open them up with my own key!" Then he raised his foot and gave a great kick that knocked a hole three full yards wide through the stones of the city wall.

In through the gap the champions went, and down by Drury Lane. They came down by the Lunnon town hall, and there stood young Lang Johnnie Mor, beside the gibbet tree.

Young Johnnie cried out, "You've come in good time, Auld Johnnie, my uncle, and Jock o' Noth, and you're unco welcome here. Come, loosen the knot and throw off the rope, and set me free from the gibbet tree."

"Nay, not so fast," Auld Johnnie said. "Why have they sentenced you to die? Is it murder you have done, or theft or robbery? If it's for a grievous crime you've been judged, it's not for us to set you free."

"Och, nay!" said young Johnnie. "For no great crime have they set me here to die. I have done no murder nor theft nor robbery. It's all because I've fallen in love with the fairest lady in Lunnon town, and that is no crime at all that I can see."

"Why did you let the soldiers take you and bind you?" asked Jock o' Noth. "And you with your good broadsword that you brought here from Scotland. I never saw a Scotsman in all my life but could free himself, as long as he had his sword in his hand."

"I had no sword in my hand," said Lang Johnnie Mor. "And if I had, I should have gone free. The de'il fly away with the king's sly rogues who put in my ale the poppy-seed oil that stole my senses away from me. But when they had me helpless and bound it took four of their stoutest men to carry my good sword away."

"Bring back the sword!" said Jock o' Noth to the king's men who were standing by. "Bring back the sword and give it back into the hand of Lang Johnnie Mor. I've one as good, if not better, of my own." And he drew his sword that all might see. "Bring back his sword and quickly, or you must answer to me, for I have sworn a black Scotsman's oath that if you delay, five thousand Englishmen will die by this sword of mine today."

The soldiers took Johnnie's shackles away, and they took the rope from around his neck and set him free. And four of the stoutest of the king's men fetched young Johnnie's sword, and put it back in his hand again.

"Now show me the lady," said Jock o' Noth. "Young Johnnie's true love, I must see."

"It's the king's own daughter that's young Johnnie's love," they said. "And she's locked in a room in the castle tower, and the king, her father, keeps the key."

Then to the king's palace went Lang Johnnie Mor, Auld Johnnie, and Jock o' Noth, all three. Through the palace door they strode and showed themselves before the king.

"Oh, where is your daughter?" roared Jock o' Noth. "That bonnie young lady I must see, for me and Auld Johnnie here have come to see her wed Lang Johnnie Mor, all the way from the foot of Benachie!"

"Oh, take my daughter!" cried the king, and his kneecaps rattled together with fear. "Take my daughter! You're welcome to her, for all of me. I never thought they bred such men at the foot of Benachie!"

"Och, if I had known," said Jock o' Noth, "that you'd wonder so much at my size, I'd have brought along another man who's at least three times as big as me. Likewise if I thought the size of me would give you such a fright, I'd have brought Sir John of Erskine Park, for he has a height of thirty feet and three."

"Let me get hold of the wee little lad who fetched you here!" cried the king. "I'll pay him well for the errand he ran, for I'll hang him with my own hands!"

"Do so!" Auld Johnnie said, and a hot fire shone in his angry eyes. "But if you do, we three, Lang Johnnie Mor, Jock o' Noth, and me, will come to the wee lad's burial, and you shall be as well paid as he, and you and the wee little lad in one same grave shall lie."

"Take the wee little lad and my daughter, too!" said the king. "And leave me be. My daughter may wed whoe'er she likes, and I shall not say nay."

"A priest! A priest!" cried Lang Johnnie Mor. "Go run for a priest and bring him here, to wed my true love and me."

"A clerk! A clerk!" the king replied. "To set down the dower my daughter will have from me."

To that Auld Johnnie Mor spoke up. "You want no clerk for we'll take no dower with your noble daughter," said he. "We've no lack of land of our own at home in Rhynie, at the foot of Benachie. We have castles and houses and farms, and our plowmen's plows are seventy-three. We've chests of gold too full to be told, and flocks and herds galore, and young Johnnie Mor has a grand estate at the foot of Benachie."

Then said Jock o' Noth to the king, "Now have you masons in Lunnon town, and any who will come at your call, that we may bring in some of them to mend the hole that I kicked in your wall?"

Said the king, "To be sure we have masons in town, and plenty to come at my call. But you can go back where you came from as fast as you can, and never mind my broken wall."

They took the key from the hand of the king, and off they went to the high stone tower. They set the king's fair daughter free, and the priest came soon, and wedded her to Lang Johnnie Mor.

There ne'er was a wedding in Lunnon town as joyful and full of glee. The merry drums beat and the merry fifes played for seven nights and seven days. Then Lang Johnnie Mor, Auld Johnnie, and Jock o' Noth, all three, they took the king's fair daughter and the wee little lad, and they all went home, to Rhynie, at the foot of Benachie.

The Tale of the
Famous Flower of Servingmen

KINGS and castles have their day and crumble into dust. But when the dust has blown away we find that they are not forever gone. The old, old tales about them still live on, and storytellers bring them back to life again. And one of the very old tales of kings and castles is the one about the famous flower of servingmen.

Long ago, in a castle in Scotland, there dwelt a bonnie young lady. She had been motherless ever since she could remember, and she was the only child of her father, a good old nobleman. Every year pushed the father a little closer to the grave, and he began to trouble himself about what was going to happen to his beloved daughter when he was no longer alive. There were no close kinsmen to look after her, she was his only heir and

would be immensely wealthy, and she was much too young to be alone in the world, having just reached her fifteenth year. The old nobleman looked about for a suitable husband for his daughter and settled his choice upon a fine young knight. With him he arranged a marriage for his daughter, and when all was done and the young couple were wedded, the old man was happy that the matter was so well settled, and not too soon, as it happened, for not much later the good old father died.

The knight carried his young bride home to his manor house in the country. She was so winsome and gentle that he loved her dearly, and he was so kind and so mindful of her happiness that she could not help loving him. He made the house fair for her, and sought to please her more and more each day, so that the two of them were as contented together as two turtledoves on a bough.

Then late one night a band of thieves came riding, and broke into the house while all inside were sound asleep. They slew the young knight before he could reach for his sword, and when the young wife screamed with horror at the sight, one of the robbers picked her up like a sack of rags and tossed her through the open window of the room.

Then the thieves went quickly through the house, ransacking it from cellar to garret until they had gathered everything of value that could be carried away. They took all the steeds and the gear from the stables, and when their booty was packed on the horses' backs, they set fire to the house. Off they galloped and left the red flames roaring behind them on the darkness of the night.

When the young wife was hurled through the window she fainted from fright. Day had begun to dawn before she came to herself and looked about her, dazed and only half-remembering what had happened during the night. By good fortune, she had fallen into a thick clump of gorse bushes that grew on the hillside below the house, far enough from the flames that she had been safe from being burned. The thick branches had caught her and broken her fall so that she was not injured, although she was badly scratched by the spiky twigs and the sharp thorns. Now that day had come she could see what damage had been done. The fire had almost consumed the walls of the manor house by then, and when she looked up and saw the smoking remains of the home where she had dwelt so happily, her heart nearly broke in two for grief. She scrambled out of the bushes and climbed the hillside to the courtyard, and there she stood with bent head, trying to gather her thoughts together and decide what she was to do.

She had no kinsmen to go to, and she had been so much alone with her father before her marriage that she had made no close friends. The servants who had remained here had all been slain by the robbers, and she was sure that those who had saved themselves by running away would not return. There was naught here for them to return to, nor was there anything left to keep her here. She was left all by herself, alone in the world. And away from here, into the world, she must go and try to find a place for herself.

Although her heart was filled with sorrow, she did not

lack courage, and she would not let herself despair. She set herself down upon the brink of the well in the court-yard and began to consider what she would have to do. She had no clothes of her own to wear except for her torn night shift which the gorse bushes had tattered into shreds. All the rest of her clothes, if not stolen, were burned to ashes in the fire. That mattered very little, she thought, for a lady could not travel about the country-side alone. She would have to go as a man. One of her husband's servingmen lay where he had fought and died in defense of his master, on the stones of the courtyard near the house. She wept to rob him, but she took away his clothes, comforting herself by thinking he needed them no longer, and in return she wrapped him as well as she could in her ragged shift. With his dagger she cut her hair short, and then she donned his doublet and hose and put his gold collar about her neck. The thieves had not noticed his sword in the darkness of the night, but now she found it and hung it at her side. The man was slight, and not tall, so the clothes did not fit too badly, but when she tried on his boots they were too big. She could not take two steps in them without tumbling head over heels, so she left them and took the buskins of her own little page, who lay dead with his head pillowed on the steps that led up to the front door. She took up the serving-man's beaver hat and set it upon her shorn head. Now, she thought, she was ready, and she must remember henceforth that she was a man, and if anyone should ask her, her name was William. So off she started to find a place for herself, and how many sighs she sighed, and how many tears she shed for sorrow, no one ever knew but herself.

Through field and forest, over moor and brae, by path and lane and highroad she traveled, and at last she came to the king's court. She went into the hall and there was the king sitting in his great chair. She bowed low to show her high respect for him.

"Stand up, my good lad," the king said, kindly. "Who are you and whence have you come?"

"My name is William and I come from the west," said she. "Your Majesty has many leal subjects in the west."

The king was pleased with her reply. He looked her over, and it never came into his mind that she was aught but what she seemed to be—a bonnie young lad with a soft voice and gentle manner, clad in travel-stained clothes. She stood before him and said in a straightforward way, "My home and all my family were put to the fire and the sword by thieves who came to our house in the night, and I am the only one left to tell the tale. I had no one to turn to, so it seemed well to come to the king and ask him to find me a place among his servingmen."

"The lad speaks well and seems to be honest," said the king to himself. "No doubt he could make himself useful here."

Then the king said aloud, "Let us hear what you can do, and if we can find a place to fit you, we will not send you away."

What would William like to be, the king asked. An usher to wait upon the king's nobles? Or an attendant at the king's table, to taste his food and wines? Or perhaps one of the castle guards to protect those in the castle? Or chamberlain of the royal chamber?

To all that he said she shook her head. "I am but a simple lad," she said. "I should fumble and be awkward waiting at table, and Heaven knows my strength would be hardly enough to protect the sparrows in the court-yard from the stable cat. These things are all too grand for me. Let me be only a plain servingman to run your small errands and make myself useful in little ways."

The king could find good use for a lad to run his little errands, so he called his nobles together to ask counsel, and they all agreed that young William o' the West was a likely lad, and he should be servingman to run errands for the king.

So the lady was given a suit of the king's livery to wear and took up her duties as a servant in the castle, and her duties were very well done. From morn to night she ran about tirelessly on errands in and out of the castle, here with a message, there with a letter, fetching and carrying willingly. It was not only the king she served, but the nobles, too, for they found her ready to do whatever they asked. If the end of the day found her weary she made no complaint, even to herself. So the deft serving-lad who smiled much but had little to say pleased them all, and soon it was that she became a favorite at the court. Sweet William was what they called the servingman—king, nobles, and all.

It was the custom of the king to go hunting each day with his nobles and their attendants in train. When they had gone, except for the servants in the kitchen, there was nobody left at home but Sweet William and an old man whom the king kept with him for charity's sake, who sat as porter at the door.

Sweet William was not unwilling to have a bit of time off from her labors. One day she came into the hall and picked up a lute that one of the king's lords had left lying upon a table. Sitting on a bench by one of the windows, Sweet William played on the lute and sang, and wept as she sang.

The old man, drawn by the plaintive melody, and curious because of the tears that flowed from the serving-man's eyes, left the door and came closer to hear the words of the song. But at once Sweet William laid the lute aside, and played no more that day.

Three times the same thing happened in the next three days, but try as he would the old man could never manage to hear the words of the song, and when the old man begged Sweet William to sing for him, the serving-man smiled and went away.

The old man's curiosity gave him no rest. He felt he must know the words of the strange, sorrowful song. So early on the next day, when the king had ridden out to the hunt, the old man hid himself behind the tapestry that hung on the wall near the window where Sweet William was wont to sit and sing. After a while Sweet William came into the hall, and seeing that the door stood open and the porter was not in sight, the serving-man picked up the lute and sang. For the first time the old man heard the song.

Sweet William sang:

My father was a noble lord,
My mother was a lady gay,
My husband was a valiant knight,
  Alas, my joys have passed away.

My friends are gone, my husband dead,
I never thought to see the day
That I should be a servingman;
  Alas, my joys have passed away.

"Husband!" said the old man to himself. "Husband?" said he, and he clapped his hands to his mouth lest he cry out in his surprise. And then he remembered that there had always been something about Sweet William that had puzzled him, although he didn't know why. But it was all clear to him now. "By the Saints!" said the old man to himself. "Our Sweet William is a bonnie young lady, and not a servingman at all!"

It was the king's way to stop at the door when he came in and say to the old man at the door. "What news, old man? What news do you have to tell me?" It was only the king's way of making the old man think he was of some importance in the castle, and not because the king expected to hear any news, for there never was any. The old man always replied. "No news, Your Majesty. No news at all today."

But this day was not as other days. "What news, old man?" asked the king as he took off his riding gloves and looked about for Sweet William to come and take them. "What news do you have for me today?"

"Braw news!" cried the old man.

"What!" cried the king in surprise.

"I have braw news to tell you," said the old man. He beckoned the king closer and whispered in his ear. "Sweet William is no servingman, nor is he a man at all! He's a bonnie young lady clad in man's attire!"

At first the king could find no words, and then he said, "Sweet William a bonnie young lady! Old man, if this be true, I'll make you a laird and settle an estate upon you, but if you have told me a lie, I'll have you hanged on the highest gibbet in the land."

But it was true, as the king found out very soon, for he went in search of Sweet William and asked her about it, and she told him the truth herself.

Then the king had the castle maids come and take away her servingman's dress, and robe her in silks and satins befitting a lady of the court, and the king himself set a crown of gold upon her head. Then he called his nobles together to give him counsel. He told them all her sad story and asked their consent to wed her and make her his queen.

Every noble in the court gave his consent most willingly, so the king married the fair young lady, and long and happily did they reign.

The old man became a laird and was given a fine estate, and many a time he was heard to say:

> "The like before was never seen,
> For a servingman to become a queen!"

The Tale of the
Heir of Linne

IN Aberdeen there was once a good old laird with an only son who was a sore trouble to him. The lad was a lightheaded, lighthearted callant, given to gambling and running hither and thither with carefree young companions like himself, and to throwing his money about on all sides. Many a time the old Laird of Linne shook his head in sorrow when he thought about his wayward son who would someday be Laird of Linne himself.

"Och, the foolish lad," the old laird would say to himself full often. "After I'm gone 'twill not be long that he'll have so much as a penny left in his pocket." But if the son would not listen to advice, what could the father do?

Well, the Laird of Linne died, and the Heir of Linne,

his son, inherited the castle, the lands, and the title, and beside, his father left him three big money chests as full of golden pounds and golden guineas as they would ever hold. The Heir of Linne mourned his father sincerely, for though he was unthrifty, still he was not unloving. But all the grief in the world would not bring his father back to him, so after a while he dried his tears and took up his life again in the old thriftless way. His days and nights were spent in revels, and the gambling rooms and the tavern knew him well. He had dozens of friends who hung upon his shoulders and told him what a fine fellow he was, with their eyes always to the gold in his pockets and their hands out for what they could get of it for themselves.

But then he was a kindhearted young man, and generous to all, from the friends with whom he caroused to the least beggar on the streets, and his money ran through his fingers like water. Three big chests hold a great lot of gold, but at the pace he was going, as might have been expected, all three were empty before much more than a year had gone by. One fine morning the Heir of Linne felt in his pockets and found nothing there. He looked in his purse and there was naught in it but a silver luck penny. He went to his money chests and opened them, one by one, and all he found was a letter in the bottom of one of the chests with his own name on it, written in his father's hand.

"Och, father!" sighed the Heir of Linne. " 'Tis no use now for you to bid me take care of my money, for there's no money left for me to take care of." Impatiently, the young laird thrust the letter, unread, into his purse and went down to the hall of his castle where his friends were waiting for him, and feasting on his food and drinking his good red wine.

Among the throng there was one who was no laird at all, but a man of low degree who, as a moneylender, had grown rich on the misfortunes of his betters, and his name was John o' the Scales. In some fashion he had managed to push himself into the company that gathered about the Heir of Linne. This John o' the Scales desired above all things to be a fine laird himself, and to own a castle and a big estate. By craft and cunning he learned that the Heir of Linne was in great need of money, so he decided the time had come for him to try for the prize he wanted so much. He whispered into the young laird's ear. "How do you fare, Laird o' Linne? Are you troubled? Is it gold that you lack? Will you not sell your lands o' Linne to such a good fellow as me?"

The young laird thought of his empty money chests, and his pockets filled with naught but air. His pretty purse had only his little silver luck penny in it, and what was the good of that? He could not keep up his lands without money. Might as well take the moneylender's gold now, and someday he would redeem them again. He took the luck penny out of his purse and threw it on the table to bind the bargain.

"I beg you all to witness, my lairds," said he, "that this penny binds a bargain made between me and John o' the Scales, who is buying my house and my lands from me."

Then John o' the Scales laid on the table, to the last penny, the money to pay for the castle and the lands of Linne.

"Take it up. The gold is yours," said John o' the Scales. "But the land is mine, and now I shall be Laird o' Linne!"

The Heir of Linne took up the gold. "Here's money enough," cried he, "for me and all my merry men!"

Before another year had passed away, all the money he got for his lands was spent, and with his gold gone, his friends departed and left him all alone.

The Heir of Linne looked into his purse and found three pennies there. But one was lead, and one was brass, and only one of the three was a true white silver coin.

"Alas," said the weary Heir of Linne. "Alas, and woe is me! I had no lack of money when I was first Laird of Linne. Now I have neither money nor lands, for I have spent the one and sold the other, and here I stand forlorn with only one little silver penny to call my own."

Then he thought of the many friends who had kept him company. "Surely there are some among them who will not forsake me," he said. "They will remember the days when they were welcome guests in my house and they will help me, now that I am in need."

From one to another he went, but in some places he stood at the door and was not let in. Some of those he had befriended in the past listened to his plea, then tossed him a gold piece or two, and told him that they were too taken up with their own affairs to give their minds to his. And there were some, among whom were those he had looked upon as his best friends, who refused to listen to him at all, and told him to go to the devil, for all they cared.

Without money, home, lands, or friends, what could the weary Heir of Linne do now? He walked down the causeway and his thoughts were bitter. He thought of his good old father who had lived well and comfortably for so many years on the yield of the lands of Linne. "God rest his soul!" cried the Heir of Linne. "Had I but heeded his counsel, I should not be forced to beg for my bread."

He took a beggar's staff and a sack for food in his hand, and walked into the town to ask alms of any who would give. As he passed by the tavern, the merry men who had once lived high at his expense looked out and saw him going by.

"Give him a glass of wine!" cried some, but some cried "Nay!" and others said that if all the beggars in the town were sentenced to be hanged, they would make sure that he would be the first to be strung up for his idleness.

When he came down to the Gallowgate and walked along the quay, he saw the fishermen there, taking their rest. There was a time when these fellows, too, had had a taste of his bounty, but when they saw him come begging among them, with his ragged clothing and his beggar's staff and sack, they began to poke fun at him.

"Give him a fish!" cried some, but others laughed loud and said, "Nay, give him a fin!" and jeering at him, they drove him away from the quay. The Heir of Linne turned himself about and went back into the town. Cold, wet, and hungry he was that sorry day. His old nurse looked out and saw him as he went plodding by the house where she dwelt. She ran out and called to him, "Come in, my bairn! Come in! Rest here a while with me, and warm yourself by my fire."

The Heir of Linne turned back and went into his nurse's house and sat down near the fire to dry his clothes, and she set food and drink out and bade him eat.

"Och, you've seen many happier days than these," she said. "And in those days you did not lack for friends."

"Give me a loaf of bread to take with me, nurse," said the Heir of Linne. "And give me a flask of wine. I will pay you back again when I am once more the Laird of Linne."

"You were once a bairn on my knee," said the nurse. "And a bonnie bairn you were. For the sake of those days I will give you a loaf of my bread and a flask of my wine, but all the seas will go dry e'er you pay them back, for you'll not be the Laird of Linne again."

The old nurse put good bread and a flask of wine in his sack, and wept to see him go out into the cheerless world again.

The Heir of Linne walked up the road to the castle that once was his own. He heard the sound of revelry inside and thought that men with such light hearts might take pity on his wretchedness. But when he knocked with his staff on the door, the porter looked out through the wicket and bade him begone and called him an idle vagabond.

The Heir of Linne sat down upon the cold stone of the step before the castle door. "If my father were still alive, he would not turn me away from his door," he sighed. "I would that he were here today to counsel and comfort me. If I had heeded his advice, I'd still be Laird of Linne, but I've learned the lesson he tried to teach too late. I'd gladly listen to him now and heed his words of advice, but it is too late."

Then, as he sat there on the cold stone, the thought came into his mind of the letter he once found in a corner of one of his empty chests. He wished now that he'd read it then, those many months before, because of the wisdom that it must have held. But where was the letter? He had put it away somewhere. He searched in his empty pockets, and in his pouch, and at last he found it in a torn place in the lining of his purse. He opened the fold of the letter and read his father's last message.

"*My son,*" he read. "*When you have come to direst need and see the folly of your ways, you may fear it is too late to recover what you have lost. When you have nothing left and no hope of anything to come, go to the one person in the world who will help you with no expectation of gain.*"

Who would help the Heir of Linne with no hope of gaining by it? Not John o' the Scales who had coveted his castle and lands and now called himself Laird of Linne. Not the young lairds who had clustered about him like flies about a honeypot while he had money, and forsaken him when he had none. Not the merry company in the tavern and the gambling rooms, and not the fishermen of the Gallowgate whom he had befriended to his cost. Only one person had helped him for love, with no hope of gain. He put his father's letter away, and took up his staff and his sack, and went to his old nurse.

He stood before her humbly. "Good nurse, I come at my father's bidding," he said. "Tell me what to do."

She saw, and did not need to ask, whether or not he rued the follies which had brought him to his sad state. She took him by the hand and drew him into her house. She led him to a small door built into the wall beneath the staircase, and put a key into his hand.

He put the key into the lock and turned it, and opened the door. He saw before him a small room which had been built into the wall. There was nothing in the room but three great chests, but when he threw back the lids he found that each chest was full of golden money to the top. At first he stood and stared, amazed at what he saw. Then his old nurse said. " 'Twas your father had the room built here, and stored the chests away until you had left your foolish ways and learned to be wise."

The Heir of Linne saw then that his father had foreseen that the wayward son must learn with pain and sorrow what the father had not been able to teach—that willful waste makes woeful want. Against that day, he had hidden half his fortune away so that his son would be able to start out in life again.

The Heir of Linne emptied his beggar's sack and set the bread and the flask of wine aside. He filled his sack with enough red gold to buy back the lands of Linne.

Then straightway along the road he went, and never stopped nor turned aside until he came again to the gate of the castle of Linne. He walked boldly in at the door, thrusting aside the porter who kept it. Into the castle hall he went and took a look at the company there.

There at the head of the table sat John o' the Scales, and his wife, in her finery, sat at the foot, while three fine lairds at either side kept the two of them company.

Then the Heir of Linne spoke up, and a saucy man was he. "My new-made laird, I'll take a cup of wine from your hand, since you do not bid me sit down with you."

Then John o' the Scales leaned back in his chair, and mockingly replied, "If the Laird o' Linne himself were standing here face to face with me, I would be the very first one to see that the laird had a seat." And full of pride at playing the laird, he began to jeer at the Heir of Linne.

Five of the lairds at the table joined in, but the sixth young callant said, "Come, man! Here are forty silver pennies for you. Come take them in your hand, and when these are gone you may come to me and I'll give you forty more. You were always a good fellow to me when you had gold to spend."

"Och, my laird," cried John o' the Scales, "I'll be as kind to the fellow as you. This beggar shall have his lands and his castle again if he likes, for one-third of the price I paid for them."

Then he tossed a penny on the table top. "Good lairds,

take witness," said he, "and the best of witnesses you will be. This penny binds the bargain should the Heir of Linne agree to buy back his lands from me."

"You've taken us for witnesses," said the lairds, "and very good witnesses we will be. But whoever buys the lands of Linne, it will not be this poor beggarman."

And John o' the Scales leaned back in his chair and laughed loud, and agreed.

But the Heir of Linne went up to the table and set upon it his beggar's sack. "I call you to witness, my nobles all," said he, "that John o' the Scales has made the bargain, and sealed it with his own penny, that I may buy back my lands and my castle of Linne for one-third of the price he paid to me."

Then he laid back the top of his beggar's sack and took out gold, and counted each piece as he laid it down, until he had taken enough from the sack to purchase back the lands of Linne.

"Now, John o' the Scales, that gold is yours. Take it up," said the Heir of Linne. "But the lands and the castle are mine. From this day I myself will be the Laird of Linne!"

"Alas!" cried the wife of John o' the Scales. "Alas, and woe is me! This morning I was the Lady o' Linne, and now I'm only John o' the Scales' wife."

"Alas!" cried John o' the Scales. "I am no longer Laird o' Linne!" He lost the title with the castle and the lands, for one-third of what he paid for them.

Then the Heir of Linne said to the good young laird who had given forty pennies to him. "Forty pennies you paid to me, but I will pay you back forty pounds. And because you have dealt fairly with me today, you shall be keeper of my forest and all within."

Then he went back down into the town, and many there were who followed him, for the lairds had spread the news around. He came to his old nurse's house and there she stood smiling by the door.

"My good old nurse," he said to her, "I'll pay you hundredfold for your loaf of bread and your flask of wine. And I vow that while you live you shall want for naught. But, good nurse, the seas still ebb and flow, and they have not gone dry, yet I am once more the Laird of Linne!"

Then the Heir of Linne, before them all, made a solemn vow that never again in his life would he endanger the lands of Linne. So he followed in the footsteps of his good old father and lived the rest of his days soberly and in comfort and ease on the yield of his lands as Laird of Linne.

The Tale of the
Knight and the Shepherd Lass

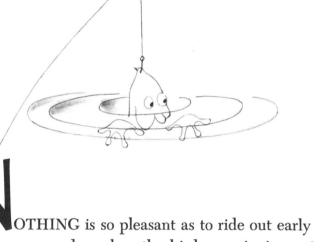

NOTHING is so pleasant as to ride out early on a sunny summer day when the birds are singing gaily in the trees, and the breeze is blowing fresh and cool, and the dew on the grass is still sparkling in the first rays of the morning sun. It was on such a day, a long, long time ago, that a gay young knight rode out through the gates of the High College to go to the court of the king. The air was bright and clear, his mind was untroubled by care, and his heart was light as he rode along, lifting his voice in a song as gay as that of the lark in the sky above. He rode the morning away, over hill and down dale, and about noontide he came to a hillside, and there he found a bonnie shepherd lass tending her ewes on the green grassy brae.

She was clad in a silken gown as green as the grass she sat upon, and she drank milk from a wee wooden bowl which she held in her two white hands. The knight pulled up his horse and bade her good day, and she looked up at him with a smile on her face. A bonnier lass he'd never seen, and it was not in his heart to be passing her by. He lighted down from his horse and let it stray among the sheep to crop the grass, while he sat down by the shepherd lass to pass a bit of time away.

"Where did you get your green silken dress?" the young knight asked the shepherd lass.

"My mother had the dress from a lady of high degree," said the lass, "and as it was not suited to her, she gave it to me."

"Are you not lonely here by yourself?" he asked.

"Nay," she answered. "Why should I be? Have I not my flock of ewes to keep me company?"

"I'll bide here with you for a while," said the knight. "Then you'll have my company, too."

"That's as you please," said the bonnie lass. But he saw by the twinkle in her eye that he was welcome to stay.

He took her hand and kissed her cheek and put his arm around her waist so trim. But she unwound his arm and took her hand away.

"If we are to be such very good friends, as you seem to think we shall be," said she, "tell me what is your name, young man, for I'd like to know who you may be."

"Some call me this, some call me that, but Ricci is my name," said the knight.

"Ricci?" she said. "Ricci?" and she said it over and over

again. "That is no Scottish name," she said. "Indeed, it has a Latin sound." The bonnie lass was learned and wise and to herself she said, "I know well what that name means. 'Tis Richard, that is this knight's true name."

"What do you know of Latin, my lass?" asked the knight. "You'd not learn Latin from your ewes."

"Och, nay!" said she. "But my father dwelt near High College once, and picked it up from the young lairds there, and all that he learned he taught to me."

He meant to stay but an hour or two, but day followed after day, and he found the lass's company too much to his taste for him to go away. He spoke of love to the bonnie lass, and promised to be true, but when she asked when they should be wed, he thought it was time to ride away.

"I've tarried here too long," he said. "So I'll bid you farewell," said he.

"But if you leave me," the lassie cried, "you'll break my heart in two!"

"Och, there are lads galore," said he, "to mend the heart of a lass as bonnie as you."

With his foot in the stirrup he leaped on his horse, and turned to ride away. She tucked her skirts above her knee, and ran along at his side. He had not enough courtesy to ask her if she'd like to ride, and she had too much pride to beg him to take her up on his horse with him. So he rode on and she ran on, all the livelong summer's day, and neither knight nor shepherd lass stopped till they came to the bank of the River Tay.

The waters ran wide and the waters ran fast, and then

he turned to the lass and said, "Lass, if you're crossing o'er the stream, will you come up and ride with me?"

"That I will not," the shepherd lass said. "For when I was still in my father's care I learned, and learned very well, when I came to deep water, to swim like any eel. And when I was still at my mother's side, I learned, and none learned better, to swim when the water runs fast, as well as any otter."

So he plunged his steed into the flood and started to ride through, and she set her lily-white feet in the water and started to cross over the stream. First she waded and then she swam, and so fast did she go that she was out on the bank on the other side before he had gone halfway.

She let down her green silken skirts and shook them out to dry, and then she sat herself down on a stone to wait till the knight had come the rest of the way.

Then the knight rode on and the lass ran on and never a word did either say, but when the day was nearly spent she came at his side to the court of the king.

She went in at the castle gate and he rode in at the other side. He went in to the stable yard, but she walked up to the castle door, and rapped, and tirled on the pin, and who came down but the king himself to let the bonnie lassie in!

She knelt and made her complaint to the king. "There's a knight in your court," said she, "who has wronged me grievously. He won my heart, then cast me aside, and broke my heart in two."

"By my troth," swore the king, "if there is a knight among my knights who has misused you so, if he be married I'll have him hanged, and if he be not married, the rogue shall either wed you or die!"

He took her hand and raised her up, "Now tell me, my bonnie lass," said he. "What is the name of the wicked knight who has treated you so cruelly?"

"Richard is his name," said the lass. "Though Ricci's the name he told to me."

"There are but three men of that name at my court, for we have Richards only three. One is old, and one is away in foreign lands, but the third is Earl Richard, the youngest brother of the queen—and how I would laugh should it happen to be he!"

"He is not old," said the shepherd lass. "Nor is he away in foreign lands, for he rode here this day with me. If you have only three knights of this name, the queen's youngest brother he must be."

Then the king put the bonnie lass at the table by his side, and they sat and waited there for all the knights to come in to dine.

"There are threescore, and maybe more, knights at my court," said the king. "Will you be able to pick him out among so many men?"

"If there were five hundred," the shepherd lass said, "I still could pick him out from the rest."

Dinner was served and all the knights and nobles came in to dine, laughing and chattering and jesting among themselves. There was only one who came in alone, lagging behind the rest, and that one was Earl Richard, the youngest brother of the queen. It had been his way in the past to push boldly forward to the head of any line. Now he came at the very end, disguised, to hide himself, as an old, old man. He limped with one leg as if lame, and blinked as if blind in one eye, and bent his back double over an old man's staff. But the eyes of the shepherd lass were too sharp to be beguiled.

"Hah-ha!" she laughed, and pointed him out to the king. "That is no old man, but Earl Richard's self I see!"

The king summoned Earl Richard to his side and the young knight put off his disguise and strode boldly to the table. Upon the table top the king laid a golden ring and a sharp shining dagger.

"There are two choices before you, Earl Richard," said the king. "You may take up the golden ring, and wed this bonnie lass. Or you may take up the dagger, and die."

Earl Richard took forty pieces of gold and put it into one of his gloves and laid it on the table in front of the shepherd lass.

"Take this gold, my bonnie lass, and find yourself another love," said he.

"I will not take your gold," said the bonnie lass. "I will have you for my husband as the king has promised me."

Then Earl Richard took forty more pieces of gold and put them with the others. "Come, take the gold," said he. "If you look about you'll be sure to find a score of men better far than me."

"I do not want your gold," she said. "I want you for my husband, as the king has promised me."

Then he laid down a hundred pounds to add to the fourscore, but the bonnie lass shook her head.

"What are your hundred pounds to me? Were they a thousand or more, they would not matter to me, when I might have for my husband the brother of the queen!"

He looked at the ring, and he looked at the knife, and the king cried, "Come! Come! You must make your choice! Will you wed, Earl Richard, or will you die?"

Earl Richard took up the golden ring. "I'll wed the shepherd lass rather than die!" said he.

The next day's morn brought their wedding day and all the king's company, the nobles, the knights, and their ladies fair, rose up early to ride to the church to see the knight wed to the shepherd lass. He would not take her up on his horse. "You shall not ride with me," said he. " 'Twould never do for a shepherd lass to ride behind the brother of a queen."

"Heigh-ho!" said she. "Then ride alone. It matters not to me, as long as the shepherd's lass is wed to the brother of the queen."

So he set himself on a milk-white steed and she set herself on a gray, and off to the church they rode with the merry wedding company. The knight pulled his hat down low on his brow to hide his face from all who might see, but his bonnie bride held her head up high, as she rode by the bridegroom's milk-white steed.

When they came out of the church again a beggar-woman stood by the door. She held out her hand and begged for alms for the sake of sweet charity. The bride put a crown in the old crone's hand. "Now, mother, run home," said she, "and tell all the folk at home that the queen's youngest brother's your son-in-law!"

"O hold your tongue, you beggar's brat!" the young knight said. "With shame you'll break my heart in two!"

"As you did mine," said the bonnie lass, "when you cast me off, back yon on the green grassy brae."

Then he rode on, on his milk-white steed, and she rode beside him on the gray.

They came to a place where, in the dike, the nettles grew rank and high. "Good day to you, you nettles tall!" cried she. "If my old mother were only here, how fast she'd pull you all! She'd pick you and pull you and chop you fine, and in her old brass pot she'd stew you well, and she would make of you a very fine mess of kail. Then she'd eat of you until she was full, and go to sleep with her head in her plate like any old barnyard sow."

"O hold your tongue, you beggar's brat!" cried the knight. "With shame you'll break my heart in two!"

"As you did mine," said the bonnie lass, "when you cast me off, back yon on the green grassy brae."

Then he rode on, on his milk-white steed, and she rode beside him on the gray.

They came to a mill by a flowing race, with the mill wheel clacketing away. "Good day to you, you bonnie wheel," said the lass. "If my old mother were only here she'd be beholden to you for many a handful of meal you've ground that she's scraped up from the floor of the mill. And she'd clean it and soak it, and boil it in her old brass pot and make it into both porridge and broth, and then all the folk in the house would eat till they were full."

"O hold your tongue, you beggar's brat!" cried the

knight. "For with shame you'll break my heart in two!"

"As you did mine," said the bonnie lass, "when you cast me off, back yon on the green grassy brae."

No wedding guests were ever so gay as the king and his company that morn. The king had ordered the wedding feast to be laid and waiting for their return in his great dining hall. The king and his lords and their ladies made merry as they sat down to dine, but the bridegroom frowned and sighed, and turned his back on his bonnie bride, and looked the other way.

The bonnie lass looked at the golden plates and cups, and at the silver spoons with which the table was laid. "Away with your golden plates and tassies!" cried she. "And go and fetch me my wee wooden bowl from which I ate, back yon on the green grassy brae. And take away your silver spoons, for they are not for me. I could never eat and enjoy my food from any but my own old cow's horn spoon."

"O hold your tongue, you beggar's brat!" said the knight. "With shame you'll break my heart in two!"

"As you did mine," said the bonnie lass, "when you cast me off, back yon on the green grassy brae."

He turned his face to the wall and wept. "I wish I had ridden by," said he, "and never stopped to dally with you, back yon on the green grassy brae."

A stranger pair you'd never see at any wedding feast. They turned their backs to each other and sat, and the bonnie bride smiled and the bridegroom wept.

A servingman stood behind each chair to serve the food and pour the wine, and the two behind the bride and the groom were talking softly together. Earl Richard heard the words they said, and thought he had not heard aright. "A match more fitting I've never seen," said one of the servingmen to the other, "than that the Scottish king's daughter should wed the queen of England's youngest brother!"

Earl Richard looked to the left, and he looked to the right, and then he turned about in his chair and looked at the bonnie lass.

"If you are the king of Scotland's daughter, as I think you may be," said he, "seven times this year I've knocked at your door, but you never would open it for me!"

"And if I refused your gold, young man," she said, "the reason you can plainly see. For every gold piece you could lay down, my father could lay three."

"But if you are not a shepherd's lass, as I'm beginning to see," said he, "what were you doing, tending the sheep, back yon on the green grassy brae?"

"I was laying a snare to catch the feet of a foolish young knight," said she.

"A foolish young knight like me," he said ruefully.

"Oh, come now! Let us forget the things that are past and start out anew!" said she.

So he took her hand and kissed her cheek, and put his arm round her waist so trim, and he saw by the twinkle in her eye that she would not take his arm away.

So in the end it all came right, and a happier wedding was never seen, than that of the king of Scotland's daughter who married the youngest brother of the English queen.